'Will entertain everyone: *Podkin One Ear*
already feels like **a classic**.'
BookTrust

'The **best book** I have ever read.'
Mariyya, age 9, Lovereading4kids

'Everything I loved from *Watership Down* . . . and *The Hobbit*. . . **a perfect present** that will ensure the reader will be curled up reading into the night.'
Minna Watson, Children's Buyer, Magrudy

'Jolly good fun.'
SFX

'I just couldn't put it down.'
Sam, age 11, Lovereading4kids

'Five stars.'
Dylan, age 12, Lovereading4kids

'Great stuff and definitely **one to watch**.'
Carabas

'**A joy to read** and absolutely **world class**.'
Alex, age 10, Lovereading4kids

'A **great** bit of storytelling.'
Andrea Reece, Lovereading4kids

About the Author

Kieran Larwood has been passionate about stories and storytelling ever since reading *The Hobbit* age six. He graduated from Southampton University with a degree in English Literature and works as a Reception teacher in a primary school. He lives on the Isle of Wight with his family, and between work, fatherhood and writing doesn't get nearly enough sleep.

About the Illustrator

David Wyatt lives in Devon. He has illustrated many novels but is also much admired for his concept and character work. He has illustrated tales by a number of high profile fantasy authors such as Diana Wynne Jones, Terry Pratchett, Philip Pullman and J. R. R. Tolkien.

THE FIVE REALMS

THE
LEGEND
OF
PODKIN
ONE-EAR

KIERAN LARWOOD
ILLUSTRATED BY DAVID WYATT

FABER & FABER

First published in 2016
by Faber & Faber Limited
Bloomsbury House,
74–77 Great Russell Street,
London WC1B 3DA
This paperback edition first published in 2017

Typeset by M Rules
Printed by CPI Group (UK) Ltd, Croydon CR0 4YY

A CIP record for this book
is available from the British Library

ISBN 978–0–571–32826–0

2 4 6 8 10 9 7 5 3 1

For Amelie

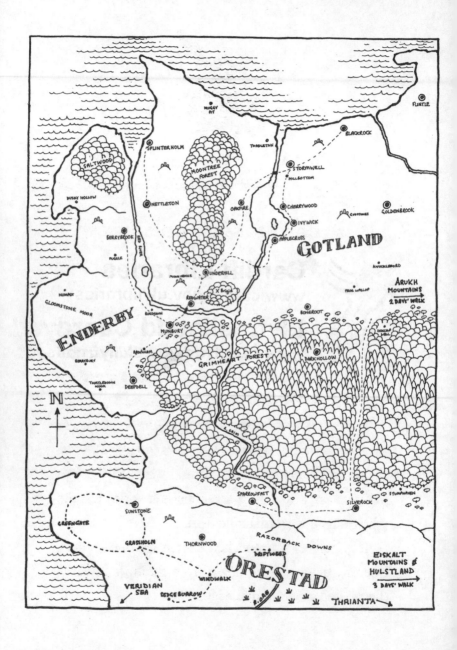

CHAPTER ONE

A Bard for Bramblemas

runch, crunch. Crunch, crunch. The sound of heavy footsteps, trudging through knee-deep snow, echoes through the night's silence.

A thick white blanket covers the wide slopes of the band of hills known as the Razorback downs. Moonlight dances over it, glinting here and there in drifts of sparkles, as if someone has sprinkled the whole scene with diamond dust.

It is perfect – untouched except for one spidery line of tracks leading down from the hills towards the frosted woodland beneath.

Crunch, crunch. Crunch, crunch go the footsteps of the track-maker. He is hunched and weary, using a tall staff to help him through the snow. He might have been an old man, if it hadn't been many hundreds of moons since men trod these lands. Move closer and instead you will see he is a rabbit, walking upright in the way men once did, his ears hidden beneath the hood of a heavy leather cloak, fierce eyes peering out at the wintry midnight world.

The thick fur on his face and arms is dyed with blue swirls and patterns, which marks him out as a bard. A travelling, storytelling rabbit. A wanderer with nothing on his back but a set of travel-worn clothes and a head stuffed full of tales and yarns: old, new, broken and mended. Just about every story you ever heard, and many more yet to be told.

Don't worry about him being out in the cold on such a wintry night. His trade will see him welcomed in any warren. That is the tradition and the law throughout all of the Five Realms of Lanica, and woe betide anyone who doesn't keep it.

Crunch, crunch. Crunch, crunch. His breath steams out behind him as he forces his way through the snow. Listen closer and you can hear him mumbling curses with each hard-fought step. Closer still and you can hear the strings of wooden beads around his neck clicking and clacking. The bone trinkets and pouches around his belt knocking and niggling.

He marches with a purpose, as if he has someplace to be and he is already late. But where is there for him to go? There is nothing but snow and trees from here all the way to the horizon. Until, of course, you remember that he's a rabbit. Rabbits live underground, in warrens and burrows: warm and safe, out of the winter ice and frost.

And that is indeed where he is heading. Into the woods and through the trees until he stops before a pair of huge entrance doors, set into the side of a little hill. Behind them is Thornwood Warren, and there had better be a warm welcome for him, or there will be serious trouble.

Boom, boom, boom! He smacks the end of his staff against the oak and waits for an answer.

Back when rabbits were small, twitchy, terrified things, warrens were little more than a collection of holes and tunnels in the ground. Now, in this new age, they are something different altogether: there are entire villages and cities built under the earth, completely out of sight.

The bard knew that behind those wooden doors would be nest-burrows and market-burrows, workshops, temples, libraries, larders, pantries and a dozen kitchens to feed them all. There would be soldiers and healers, servants, cooks, smiths, weavers, tailors, potters and painters. Old rabbits, young rabbits, poor rabbits and noble rabbits. All walks of life hidden away in cosy, torch-lit, underground houses; all arranged around every warren's hub: the longburrow, a great feasting hall with a huge fireplace, rows of tables and nearly always music. Music, noise and merriness – that is what rabbits love. Especially tonight, for this was Bramblemas Eve: the night on which the winter solstice was celebrated with a special feast, and the promise of presents in the morning, left behind by the mysterious Midwinter Rabbit.

And stories of course. Special stories, told by a visiting bard – that is, if he ever got inside the place.

Boom, boom, boom! He smacks the doors again and is about to do so a third time when he hears a muffled voice on the other side.

'All right, all right, keep your ears on, I'm coming!' There are more words about stupid people being outside on this kind of night, but luckily the heavy wood absorbs most of those. Finally, the doors creak open, spilling golden torchlight on to the snow, and the face of a burly soldier-rabbit pokes out.

'Who in the Goddess's name are you?' he says, glaring at the stranger. Underneath the hood, the pale green eyes glare back.

'Is that any way to treat a bard, come to tell tales on the Eve of Bramblemas? Is that how the old ways are kept here at Thornwood?'

Even though the soldier-rabbit is the size of a small armour-clad mountain, something about the bard makes him tremble a little. 'Sorry, sir,' he says, and pushes the door open further with his shoulder. 'Come in and share our hearth on this Middlewinter night . . .'

'*Mid*winter, turnip-head,' corrects the bard, stepping into the torchlight and the warmth. The warren doors close behind him, and he shakes the snow from his cloak with a shudder. 'Now. Which way to the fireside?' And he strides off down the paved entrance hall as if he has been here a hundred times before.

'What's a Midwinter Turnip-head then?' mumbles the puzzled guard, before turning to trot after him.

*

Just as every warren is carefully built around the longburrow at its centre, the rabbits inside are organised around their chieftain. He is the leader of the tribe, just as his father was before him, and his son will be after. Between him and his wife, all the warren decisions are made, all the arguments settled and all the feasts and festivals organised.

In Thornwood, the chieftain is Hubert the Broad. A great big-bellied lop rabbit, with brown and white patched fur, ears down to his knees and a stomach you could build a house on. He is currently sitting on his throne at the head of the feasting table, a bramble crown on his head and his great piebald stomach bursting the seams of his tunic. He is singing a merry song about the Midwinter Rabbit getting stuck in his burrow, while all the little rabbits sit laughing at his feet. When he sees the bard enter, he stops, stands and raises his drinking horn in salute.

'Welcome, bard!' he shouts, in a voice that shakes earth from the ceiling. 'Welcome, on Bramblemas Eve!'

'That's more like it,' mutters the bard, shrugging off his leather cloak. He keeps his hood on, but the light from the fire still shows off the swirls and whorls of blue patterns dyed into the fur on his bare arms.

'We thought you weren't coming,' says Hubert. 'But Bramblemas Eve is full of surprises. Will you sing for your supper?'

The bard chuckles. 'My voice is too old and cracked for singing.' He takes a seat by the fireside and warms his hands. 'But I might be persuaded to tell a tale or two.'

'Bring this man some food! Quick, sharp,' Hubert shouts, flicking his ears at his cupbearers. They scurry off and return moments later with a bowl of buttery turnip soup and a platter of cornbread. The bard tucks into it like a rabbit starved and, finishing it, wipes his mouth with the back of his paw.

'I suppose that deserves a tale,' he says. 'What would you like to hear?'

The little rabbits swarm to his feet, all crying out at once. 'Beobunny!' 'The Fisher Rabbit!' 'Podkin One-Ear!'

'Did I hear someone mention Podkin One-Ear?' says the bard, settling further into his chair. 'Podkin the Horned King? The Moonstrider? Podkin of the magic knife?' When the little ones nod their heads and shriek with excitement, he folds his painted arms and tugs at his beard.

'I do know some tales of that one, but they will be different from those *you* have heard. Nothing about shooting fire from his eyes or wrestling giant rabbits with bare hands. Nothing like that at all.'

'What kind of tales, bard?' 'Why are they different?' 'Why won't there be fiery eyes and giants?'

'They're different,' he says, 'because they are *true*. And because fiery eyes don't exist anywhere except in fairy tales and the heads of silly young rabbits.' The bard waves a hand for silence, and then he begins.

CHAPTER TWO

The Worst Bramblemas Ever

The Gorm. First, you need to know about *them*.

Nowadays, thank the Goddess, they are nothing but a bad memory. Something to scare the little ones with at night. But back when your grandparents were young, rabbits lived in constant fear of their strange riders, of the screeching of metal in the night and the echoing of their terrifying war-horns.

The Gorm.

Nobody knows exactly how they came to exist, only that they were first seen in a little warren called

Sandywell, up in northern Enderby, where the Red River meets the sea.

A meek little tribe of rabbits lived there. Grey-furred sable bunnies that liked fishing, sailing and building boats. They never caused any trouble, and nobody paid them much attention. Until, one day – everything changed.

Some say there was something in the river that got into their veins. Some say they tunnelled too far down and came across something cursed and poisonous. Others say it was the work of witches. Whatever the reason, they stopped being the Sandywell greys overnight, and turned into something else. Something evil and unnatural.

First the warren changed – just a little at first – until eventually great spikes of jutting metal burst out of it, sticking up into the air like poison porcupine quills, and the land around became blackened and scorched. The waters of the Red River turned black and noxious as they ran past. Animals that lived in the woods and waters either died or became warped and ruined. Folk started calling the warren Splinterholm and stayed well away. But that didn't help them.

Next, the old Sandywell rabbits reappeared, except now you wouldn't have recognised them. They were clad head to foot in iron armour. Iron – that metal that rabbits find impossible to work with, and poisonous to the Goddess herself.

The Sandywell rabbits had not only shaped and moulded it; they had bonded with it somehow. It seemed as though the metal had fused and pierced their very skin. It ran through their veins and bled into their eyes, turning them blank and rusty red. The rabbits used the metal to bend and shape the creatures around them as well: the dumb giant rats that all rabbits use as beasts of burden, and the black crows of the nearby woods. They changed *them* into shrieking flocks of rusted metal harpies.

When they rode out of Splinterholm, they came to devour and destroy, and they were called the Gorm by all who feared them.

If they called at your warren, then that was the end of you – they would kill your chieftain and his sons. They would rip your warriors into shreds. Then they would carry half of you off to be *changed* into Goddess-knows what. The rest would spend their miserable lives making food and supplies to feed their new masters, never knowing when they too would be dragged away, wailing in the night.

It was a dark time for all rabbitkind, is what I'm saying.

It was in those days that Podkin One-Ear lived. He wasn't a hero back then: he hadn't slain any giant rabbits, or formed any robber bands, and he hadn't even begun to think about rescuing maidens. In fact, he was only a youngling; eight summers' old. Oh, and he still had both his ears.

Podkin was the son of Lopkin, chieftain of the Munbury warren, which meant that someday he himself would be chieftain, just like his father's father had been, and *his* father ... all the way back to when the Goddess first made the twelve tribes. For now, that all seemed a long way off, and that was the way he liked it.

He had an older sister called Paz, who liked to boss him around as much as possible, and a young kitten of a brother called Pook, who didn't do much except chew things and ask for soup.

You might think as a young rabbit that Podkin

was already showing signs of heroism: great skill with a sword, maybe. Bravery, courage, wisdom, determination.

You would be wrong.

If anything, he was perhaps the laziest, most spoilt son of a chieftain in the whole Five Realms! At least he was, up until the start of this story. His father tried his best to prepare him for leadership with lessons in history, rabbit-lore and soldiering, but Podkin took great delight in avoiding them all. Daydreaming and snoozing were the only things he practised and, to be fair, he was very good at them. He was the despair of all his tutors, especially poor Melfry, the weaponmaster, who resigned three times or more from the task of teaching Podkin. The young rabbit simply had no interest in doing what was expected of him.

So it came to pass, that on a Bramblemas Eve – much like this one – Podkin One-Ear (although technically Two-Ears at this point) was sitting upstairs in the wooden gallery that ran around the edge of Munbury longburrow. He was lazily pushing around a toy wagon, munching on a stolen piece of cornbread and daydreaming about the Midwinter Rabbit, who would be visiting that night (hopefully with a sackful of presents). Would he get the wooden soldiers he'd asked for? Or the toy sword and shield? Or would it be the disappointment of a badly knitted woollen tunic, like last year?

'What are you doing up here, Pod?' His sister had tiptoed up the stairs and was now glaring at him. Podkin's little brother Pook was nestled in the crook of her arm, chewing away at a carrot. 'Mother sent me to get you. They're about to have turnip soup and dance the Bramble Reel. You should be there, seeing as you're next in line to be *chief.*'

Paz took it hard that she was never going to lead the warren, even though she was the eldest. But it was tradition, fair or not, that the first son took over.

Podkin yawned deliberately. 'The Bramble Reel. How exciting.' He took Pook from her and tickled his tummy. He could hear all the festivities in the hall below, and had absolutely no desire to join in with them. 'Please stand aside, so I can rush down the stairs and prance about like a prize pudding.'

'If you don't come down, you're going to be in trouble,' said Paz. 'Do you have any idea what it takes to be chieftain? Nobody will want to follow a lord who spends all his time tickling his baby brother, playing with toys and hiding away in corners daydreaming.'

Podkin huffed and flicked his ears at his sister. 'You're just jealous because you think you would make a better chieftain than me.'

'Well, I would, wouldn't I? Anyone can see that.' Paz started ticking off a list on her fingers. 'I'm the eldest. I do what Father and Mother tell me. I go to all my lessons, instead of hiding in the meadow and picking daisies like a rat-brained, fairy flump. If there was any justice, girls would be allowed to become a Chief, instead of brats like you who don't deserve it!'

Podkin was about to leap on Paz and pull her ears, when the warren horn began to sound. The three young rabbits rushed to the edge of the gallery and looked down on to the hall. Soldiers were grabbing spears and shields, children were being herded into the corners and their father, Chief Lopkin, was striding towards the burrow entrance, drawing his sword. His great silver broadsword that evcryone thought was magical.

'Mi'winter wabbit! Mi'winter wabbit!' Pook shouted, trying to wriggle free.

'It's not the Midwinter Rabbit, Pook,' said Podkin, the argument with Paz forgotten. 'It looks like trouble. And trouble doesn't leave presents outside your burrow at night.'

Frightened murmurs were drifting up from the crowd below. 'A rider', 'a lone rider coming', and then 'a rider wearing armour ... *iron* armour', and finally 'it's the Gorm! The Gorm are here!'

This last shout caused mass panic. Podkin could see his father shouting, but his voice was swallowed up by the hubbub. The warren was terrified, losing its head. This was the time it really needed its chieftain: somebody to *lead* them all. Pod watched Lopkin breathe deep, then bellow in his great commanding voice: '*Silence!*'

The whole longburrow instantly froze, hundreds of scared eyes turning to Lopkin who stood amongst them, his magic silver sword flashing. He let the silence stand for a moment before speaking in as calm a voice as he could.

'A rider approaches, true. A Gorm, true. But it is a lone rider, and he carries the white flag of peace. We will let him enter and see what he has to say.'

The sound of the heavy oak entrance doors opening echoed down the warren. The rabbits in the longburrow pressed back against the walls. Spears were raised, breath was held. Something was making its way along the entrance hall.

'Will it be okay, Paz?' whispered Podkin. He had always been in awe of his tall, powerful father. He had always seemed invincible – at least until now.

'I don't know, Pod,' Paz replied. 'Father has his sword ...'

The look in her eyes was enough to make Podkin truly afraid for the first time in his short life.

Chief Lopkin called out the traditional greeting to the darkness of the tunnel. 'Enter, stranger, and be welcome on this Bramblemas Eve.'

Clank.

Screeeeeech.

Grinding metal, followed by the clump of heavy leather boots. It seemed the rider had dismounted whatever had been carrying him and was now coming down the entrance tunnel on foot. One hundred and fifty terrified rabbits all held their breath.

Clank.

Screeeeeech.

Pook began whimpering. They could now see something moving in the darkness of the tunnel. Torchlight from the great hall caught on metal and bounced back in orange glints.

'Enter!' Lopkin called out again. 'We mean you no harm!'

With a final grinding squeal, the figure emerged and leapt from the tunnel to land in the centre of the warrior's circle.

The rabbits had all heard terrifying tales of the Gorm, but none had done the real thing justice.

This wasn't a rabbit any more. If it ever had been, it was now something else entirely. A walking slab of metal and meat, pierced through with rusty thorns and nails. Its armour overlapped in sheets of jagged, dented iron; mottled with rust and splashes of dried crimson that looked very much like old blood.

Its head was completely covered by a helm, dotted all over with cruel shard-like spikes and curved metal horns that almost scraped the ceiling. From the shadowy eye slits, two dim scarlet pupils glowed: blank and mottled with rusty red veins.

Podkin was so scared, he wanted to cry. Worst of all was the thing's jagged black iron sword. That and the skulls that hung from its belt. Rabbit skulls, painted all over with evil-looking runes. Skulls of all sizes, including ones that looked like children's.

The Gorm rabbit turned his head to and fro, taking in the warren's inhabitants, before resting his gaze on Lopkin himself.

'I don't want your welcome.' The deep voice echoed inside its iron shell. A cold, iron, killer's voice. 'I came to tell you I am taking your warren. That, and your magic weapon.'

Instantly, every spear was raised and pointed at the armoured intruder. The Gorm tilted his head slightly, as if curious, and leant over to thump his sword three times on the floor.

There was a rumbling, deep below the ground.

The whole floor of the longburrow began to shake, and then parts of it started to crack and crumble. The Munbury rabbits backed against the walls, as piles of mud burst upwards, shattering the tiled floors and overturning benches and tables. From beneath the ground, armoured Gorm began to clamber out into their midst. Pushing their way up through the soil, spilling torrents of mud from their spiked iron shoulders, as the Munbury rabbits stared on in mute horror. Five, ten, fifteen of them and more, each one clad head to foot in jagged rusty armour and wielding an axe or sword.

'This warren is ours now,' said the first Gorm, his voice like the metallic screeching of his armour. 'And we will kill anyone who thinks otherwise. So says the chief of all the Gorm.'

'Scramashank,' said Chief Lopkin. The Gorm Lord's name was well known amongst rabbits, and well feared.

Lopkin raised his silver sword and stepped into a battle stance. 'Scramashank – leave my people out of this. We will settle this between the two of us.'

'They aren't your people any more.' Scramashank

laughed, as if this were all some elaborate Bramblemas joke. 'They are the Gorm now. Or they will be. Once you are dead.'

In a flash of iron, Scramashank swung his sword over his head and down, trying to cleave Lopkin in half. The chieftain raised his silver sword just in time, and there was an almighty *clang* as the blades clashed, showering sparks about the hall.

'Father!' Podkin and Paz both screamed out at the same time. Pook began to bawl and wail.

They had a brief glimpse of Lopkin gazing up at them, Scramashank drawing back for another blow, and then they were pulled back, away from the gallery rail.

All three young rabbits shrieked, expecting to see a Gorm standing behind them, but instead it was their Auntie Olwyn. Tears had dampened the fur around her eyes, but her jaw was set and fierce.

'Come with me, you three.' She pulled them back towards the stairs.

'But, Father ...' Podkin began.

'Don't think about him. He has to fend for himself.' She was dragging them down the stairway.

'You have to leave with me *now*. Before the Gorm come for you too.'

She was too strong to resist, and even as the sound of shouts and clashing metal began to echo up from the longburrow, the little rabbits ran with their aunt through the Munbury tunnels. Twisting this way and that, they soon ended up at their parents' bedchamber.

'In here,' whispered Auntie Olwyn, shoving them inside and barring the door behind them. She ran straight to the bed and began rummaging around underneath it.

'What are you *doing*, Auntie? We have to go back! We have to help Father!'

'There's no helping him now. He'll soon be in the Land Beyond, Goddess save him,' she said, under her breath. She stood up, holding something long and thin, wrapped in cloth. She thrust it into Podkin's hands.

'Your father told me to give you this, should anything ever happen to him. And your mother told me to bring you here, if the warren should ever fall.'

'To the bedroom?' Paz looked at her aunt as if she had gone suddenly mad. Podkin was peeking under the cloth bindings. They hid a battered old copper dagger, dull and blunt with a crude face carved on the pommel.

'There's a secret tunnel here.' Olwyn pulled on the bedpost and a little door slowly opened in the wall. She gave each of the children a quick kiss on the forehead. 'Go now,' she said. 'Get out of the tunnel and run as fast as you can. Get to Redwater warren and ask for help there. Don't even *think* of coming back here. Not ever.'

'But what about you? What about Mother?' Podkin asked.

'Don't worry about us. We'll be all right. And if not, we'll see you in the Land Beyond. Remember, children: your parents love you. They love you so very much.'

With that, she bundled them into the tunnel and then, before they could do anything about it, she shut the door behind them and locked it tight.

CHAPTER THREE

Starclaw

I don't need to go into detail about that awful flight out of the dark tunnel, about how the three of them sobbed and wailed their way to the surface, and out into the snowy woods. Or about how they ran through the rest of that dark, blizzard-choked night, terrified that every shadow hid an enemy, that every second could be their last on this miserable earth.

You don't need to know how many times they thought about going back, of trying somehow to save their mother or their aunt or their friends. Or how often each one of them stumbled to the ground, overcome with grief, until the other pulled them up and onwards again.

That terrible night can only really be remembered by those two poor little rabbits (Pook was thankfully too young to know what was going on beyond being cold, hungry and away from his mother) and neither of them will ever speak of it again – not even to each other.

All you need to know is that, as the sky began to lighten in the east, the young rabbits staggered into a clearing and finally rested against the trunk of an old frost-covered oak.

'W-where do you think we are?' stammered Podkin. 'Are we anywhere near Redwater?'

'How am I supposed to know?' said Paz. Pook was nestled inside her tunic, the only one of them feeling slightly warm. 'I was lost five minutes after we came out of the tunnel. Maybe if you'd paid attention in our geography lessons . . .'

'*You* were paying attention for me! And you don't know where we are either, so the lessons were a fat waste of both our time, weren't they?'

Neither of them spoke for several minutes. They

knew how serious it was to be lost in the woods in this weather. The cold was deadly, and there were hungry wolves and bears around, not to mention the Gorm.

'I think we should ...' began Paz, but she was interrupted by an explosion of fluttering overhead. A large bird flapped its way up through the falling snow and away over the trees. 'Just a crow,' she said, relieved. 'I thought it might be ... you know ...'

'Not just a crow,' whispered Podkin. 'It was one of them. Didn't you see? It had metal spikes bursting through its skin. And its eyes ... its eyes were like theirs ...'

'You're imagining things, Pod. After what happened ... your mind isn't working properly.'

'It is! I *saw* it!'

'A crow? How can a crow be like them?'

'Don't you remember Father saying?' Podkin was crying again now: big fat tears that splashed down to melt holes in the snow. 'They change things. Things like crows and rats. They turn them into their servants. That crow spotted us, and it'll tell them where we are.'

Paz still wasn't convinced, but they had to keep moving. Hoping all the time that they would see something to give them a clue as to where they were. If only everything wasn't covered in so much cursed snow.

Paz shifted the sleeping lump inside her tunic that was Pook, and started to move off again, only to notice Podkin wasn't following. He had his nose stuck in the cloth-wrapped bundle that Auntie Olwyn had given him. 'Come *on*, Podkin! We have to get moving!'

But Podkin wasn't budging. 'Wait a minute, Paz. There's something here.'

Podkin hadn't paid much attention to the dagger all night. In fact, he had been using it as a walking stick to help pull himself through the snow, and had half forgotten he had it at all. But now that there was some dawn light, he was curious as to why it was so special, and a quick peek had revealed a piece of parchment wrapped around the blade. He pulled it out.

'It's a message.' He handed it to Paz. 'Here, you look. I can't read Ogham.'

As I'm sure you will all know, Ogham is an ancient written language and was designed for simple marking of posts, trees and standing stones. Podkin had always been too lazy to learn it, much like everything else, although now he was sorely regretting it.

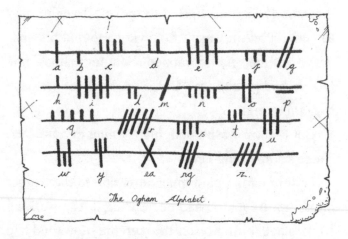

The Ogham Alphabet.

Paz stared at the parchment for a few seconds, her breath steaming around her head in a cloud as she gasped. 'It's a letter from Mother.'

My darlings. If you are reading this, then our worst nightmares have come true, and the Gorm have come to Munbury. Thank the

Goddess that you have escaped. This dagger
you are holding is our warren's greatest
treasure: the magical dagger known as
Starclaw. Your father lets everyone think that
his silver broadsword is the magic weapon,
but it has always been this simple copper
knife. It is one of the Twelve Gifts given to
the first tribes back at the start of time. It
may not look special, but it has the power
to cut through anything. Anything, that is,
except iron.

We know the Gorm are hunting the Twelve
Gifts for some evil reason, so this dagger
must be kept from them at all costs. That is
now your job.

Run fast, my darlings, and run far. Your
father and I love you more than you will ever
know. Mother.

If Paz hadn't already cried out every last tear in her
body, she would have started sobbing again. Instead
she stood, numb both inside and out, staring at the
copper dagger in Podkin's hands.

All Podkin could think to say was, 'What use is a magic dagger that doesn't cut iron against a load of iron-armoured warriors?'

'What were you thinking of doing with it, genius? Storming back and chopping the Gorm to bits?'

Podkin shrugged. 'It is a *magic* weapon.'

'But we're not heroes out of some story. We're just children.'

Podkin stared at the dagger again. A useless hunk of metal, and yet so precious to the Gorm that his father had to die for it. He was so upset and confused he felt like flinging it away into the snow.

Only his mother's plea stopped him. Would he ever see her again? He tried to think of the last words she had said to him, the last time he had hugged her, but he couldn't remember. It suddenly seemed so important, but his mind was frozen blank.

'Run fast, my darlings, run far.' That would have to do instead. He would keep hold of the dagger for her sake. He rolled it and the parchment back into the blanket and looked up at his sister.

'Well, what shall we do then? We don't even know where we are!'

'Redwater is north-east. The sun is rising in the east. We head that way.'

Podkin didn't feel as if he could go another step, let alone run all the way to Redwater. He was about to argue some more when he thought he heard a noise in the distant woods.

The rabbits pricked their ears, listening for something in the heavy silence of the falling snow. In amongst the muffled forest sounds and Pook's wheezy little snores, they heard it again: a sound that made their blood run cold (well, cold*er* – it was already almost frozen).

Somewhere far behind them, but growing louder very quickly, was the echoing wail of a strange horn. And behind that was another, quieter sound. The clanking, scraping of iron against iron.

CHAPTER FOUR

Timber!

If there's one thing rabbits are good at, it's running away. It goes back to the days when we were tiny tasty bundles of fluff: top of everyone's menu, and afraid of our own shadows. The slightest hint of danger, and we'd be scurrying for shelter before we became breakfast for something with sharp teeth and an appetite.

But Podkin and Paz had already done their fair share of running that long cold night. Their muscles were torn and aching, their fur matted with clods of frozen snow. Paz's arms were weary from carrying Pook, even though he was only a little bundle. The best they could manage was a kind of panicky stumble, on through the trees and away from the sounds of the oncoming Gorm. Those terrible wrenching sounds that were getting closer by the heartbeat.

Paz hoisted Pook further up with a grunt, ignoring his little squeal of protest. 'We need to run faster, Podkin!'

'I'm going as fast as I can,' Podkin managed to gasp.

If Podkin had had the energy, he would have grumbled some more, but it was all he could do to keep moving. They struggled on, wading through the snow, until they found themselves faced by a wall of earth and tree roots. There were banks on either side of them too. In their panic they had dashed into a cranny: a scooped-out section of the forest floor, hidden beneath the swathes of drifted snow.

From the trees behind them came the screeching of jagged metal armour. The Gorm were close now – minutes away, seconds even.

Podkin stared around, eyes wide with terror.

'We're dead,' he whispered, his voice harsh and strangled. 'There's no way out. They're going to kill us, just like they did Father.'

'Shut up! You're scaring Pook.' Paz pulled her tunic tighter around the baby rabbit, who was starting to squeak with fear.

'Well, what else is going to happen? How can we get away?'

Paz stood still for a moment. Her brain was whizzing, trying to come up with an idea that would save them. She was good under pressure, but there had never been pressure quite like this before. 'It did say that dagger could cut through anything except iron, didn't it?' she said. Podkin nodded.

'Right then.' It wasn't much of an idea, but it would have to do. She grabbed Podkin and whispered into his ear.

*

Half a minute later, after a desperate scramble up the cranny side, Podkin stood hidden behind a tree. With shivering paws, he unwrapped the cloth bundle and drew out the copper dagger.

It should have been cold metal, as icy as the snow

around him, but instead the hilt was hot – tingling almost. Could that be the magic? Would it really cut through anything? It certainly *felt* powerful. Not like the wooden practice swords he used to use in his boring weapons lessons.

Podkin swished it through the air a few times. Just a dagger, but to him it was more like a short sword, although he didn't feel much of a soldier. Certainly nothing like his father: facing down the Gorm Lord all on his own. *Father.* Was he looking down on them now, from the Land Beyond, or wherever he might be? Would he try and help them somehow, or would he only be able to watch them die? *Now is not the time for this*, Podkin told himself. They had a plan. He had a job to do.

Below him cowered Paz, out in plain sight, backed up against the bank of tree roots. She was clutching Pook to her chest and looking suitably terrified. Bait for their hastily assembled trap.

From his hiding place, Podkin could hear the Gorm, riding through the forest on their mounts. They were heavy, lumbering things, smashing against saplings and branches and ploughing the snow aside with brute force. He could hear the tortured creatures breathing and growling; he could hear the slow grinding of armoured plates sliding against one another.

Pod held the dagger hilt close to his face and gave a small prayer to the Goddess. Should he do it now? *No*, he told himself. *Better to have a peek first. The timing must be right.*

Podkin never wanted to see another Gorm in his life, but he forced himself to peer around the tree trunk. There were two of them: riders sitting on top of things that might once have been giant rats.

Rats were normally docile, fluffy, stupid creatures that spent most of their time eating and squeaking. These looked as though they had been forged from shards of rusted iron, pounded together in the blacksmith's of hell.

They were covered all over with plates of jagged metal, studded with spikes and hooks, and scrawled on in blood-red runes. At the front, where their heads should have been, were fanged, drooling mouths, and glaring out from holes in the armour were blank rust-red eyes. They weren't rats any more. Every part of them, down to their bones, had been changed and twisted. These things were now beasts. Iron beasts. Monsters.

They clanked and shrieked their way along the little track of footprints that Paz had left, their riders leaning forward on their backs, gnashing their teeth with hunger. They looked as if they had grown out of their mounts' spines, or been fused together into some new horrid form of life.

A voice came then. Sharp and loud, it sounded like sheets of tin being ripped into shreds. 'You! Girl! Where is your brother? Where is the chieftain's son?'

Podkin heard Paz say something, but it was too weak and stuttering to make out. Could it be she was terrified speechless, or was she just luring the Gorm riders in? That was the sort of clever trick she would try. Podkin remembered all the wily things she would do to taunt and tease him back in the warren. Nasty names and embarrassing pranks. He used to hate her sneaky cleverness then, but now he silently thanked the Goddess for it.

'Speak up, you little runt!'

The rider's voice sounded very close to Podkin. With small, silent steps, he edged around the tree trunk.

The two riders were right below him now. He could see the little pits and scratches on the surface of their armour. He could smell the hot iron stink of their steaming breath.

Now. Do it now!

He remembered being shown how to chop down a tree, back when his father was trying to teach him to do chores. He hadn't really listened because why should a chieftain's son have to do hard work? Now he really wished he had paid more attention. *Something about cutting out a wedge ...*

He almost had to shout at his frozen, terrified body to make it respond. Tearing his eyes away from the Gorm, he set the edge of the dagger against the tree trunk. The blade was blunt tarnished copper, marked with notches and dents. It made him doubt the magic. There was no way it would even make a mark on the wood, let alone cut through it. Why had he listened to Paz's stupid idea?

Podkin held his breath, teeth gritted. If the riders

looked up and saw him now, it was all over. He had to get this done – and quick. He moved the blade up the trunk and angled it downwards. Holding his breath, he pushed it into the bark.

He half expected nothing to happen, so when it did, he was shocked dumb. The dagger slid through the hundred-year-old oak like it was butter. Podkin only just managed to stop it before it came out the other side.

Now the upwards cut. Quick!

Podkin pulled the dagger out and made another cut from the bottom up. A thick triangle of wood dropped out and thudded into the snowy ground. Down below, the riders were slinking forward; Paz was still stammering something about losing her brother in the snow. And then came a low, groaning sound that made Podkin's ears judder. It took a moment for him to realise it was coming from the oak tree as it began to topple forward. Slowly at first, but picking up speed, cracking and snapping branches as it fell. Pod saw the Gorm riders look up, surprised clouds of breath gushing from behind their iron masks, and then the tree hit them with an explosion of snow crystals and a roar that echoed through the forest.

It took several moments for the snow clouds to settle, for the echoes to bounce away into silence. When all was quiet again, Pod peered down into the cranny and saw the great oak trunk snapped in half, blocking the whole thing. Snow crust lay crumbled and piled around it. Of the riders, nothing could be seen except a twisted shard of armour and a splash of rusty crimson blood on the snow.

INTERLUDE

The bard stops talking and gazes in Chief
Hubert's direction, smacking his lips and
generally trying his best to look thirsty. Hubert
takes the hint and flicks an ear at his dozing
cupbearer, so hard it nearly knocks him backwards.
The startled rabbit grabs a wooden flagon, filled to
the brim with frothy honey mead and dashes over
to the storyteller. Amongst protesting cries from
the little rabbits sitting around his feet, the bard
drains the whole flagon in three long gulps, and
then wipes the froth from his beard with the back
of his hand.

'Don't stop! Don't stop!' the rabbits cry. 'Tell us
what happened next!'

The bard lets out a belch, frowns, then lets out
another. 'Give me a minute,' he says. 'My pipes don't

work as well as they used to. Bless my turnips, that was good mead.'

'Were the Gorm really real?' one little rabbit asks. 'My brother said they were just made up to frighten baby bunnies at night.'

'They were ... *burp* ... really real,' replies the bard. 'Excuse me.' He eyes a plate of fresh steaming cornbread, next to a huge bowl of turnip soup, a knob of creamy butter slowly melting in its centre. But his audience have no intention of letting him stop for much longer.

'What do you think it was that changed them then? Did anyone ever find out? Was it the witch's curse, or was it something else?' The fear in the little rabbit's eyes makes it all too clear she is worrying that the same thing might happen in Thornwood.

'Could've been a curse,' says the bard. 'Could've been something much more horrible. As far as *this* part of the story goes ... Ooh dear. I *really* shouldn't gulp my drink like that ... As far as this part of the story goes, nobody had any idea. That's all you need to know for now.'

The bard is about to carry on, but something in the little rabbit's eyes makes him stop. Wide, white and terrified, with tears glistening in the corners. He likes to scare his audience a little, but this is Bramblemas Eve. She should be going to bed with dreams of sugared carrots and carved wooden dollies, not lying awake, scared witless.

He tugs his beard a few times, then reaches into one of the pouches on his belt, bringing out an ancient, much-folded piece of leather.

'Listen,' he says. 'I don't normally do this, but . . .'

'What?' the rabbits all squeal. 'What have you got there?'

'This?' says the bard, unfolding the stained leather. 'This is something I found on my travels. Something I don't usually read out to children. Especially not when I'm in the middle of a tale.'

'Oh please read it! *Please.*' The little rabbits are desperate for something secret, something forbidden.

'It's an account, you see. A tale of its own, copied down word for word from this old rabbit I met, far to the east of here, in Hulstland.' The bard holds up the leather to show rows and rows of tiny runes, burnt or inked into it. The rabbits all kneel up to squint at it, even though most of them can't yet read.

'A tale of what? The Gorm? How they were made?'

'Rhubarb and radishes, but you are nosy ones! Yes. How the Gorm came to be, in the words of one that was there. Now, I'll read it to you, but only if you promise to remember where we got to in the story. Do we have a deal?'

The rabbits all shout about how well they can remember, and that the deal has definitely been made. Nodding and waving at them to shush, the bard spreads the leather out on his knee and begins to read.

My name is Auna. I am old now – a longtooth as they say here in Hulstland – but once I was a young rabbit, born in a little warren on the northern coast of Enderby called Sandywell. A simple place, full of simple grey-furred fisher-rabbits.

That warren has another name now, and the rabbits don't fish any more. Now they are called the Gorm, and they do things that set your fur shivering and your ears shaking. But it wasn't always that way. That's why I want my story written down: so that others can learn from it. So that the same thing doesn't happen to any other warren like it did ours.

When I was a little doe, we had a happy, carefree life. We lived right on the edge of the sandiest beach you ever saw, and we used to spend hours running around the dunes and splashing in the rock pools.

When I think back, all I remember is the sun in my eyes, sand between my toes and salt spray on my fur. Happy days.

Our chief was a funny little rabbit named Crama. Crama the Cautious, he was known as, for he never made a decision without going over it a hundred times or more. He was known for changing his mind, getting muddled and generally putting everything in a pickle.

I remember hearing my father and his friends moaning about him many an evening in the longburrow, but nobody dared do anything about it. He had the magic helmet of the Goddess, you see. A great metal thing with copper horns. On him it looked like an upside-down cauldron, but it protected him from any spear or blade, and he never took it off. It did have a special name, but we just called it 'the Copperpot'.

Sandywell wasn't the most exciting warren to live in, but it was safe and warm and we were happy. At least until that terrible day.

I don't like to speak of it, but I know I must.

Crama, our chief, had finally decided that we needed to dig a new longburrow. The sandy soil of the warren tended to crumble, and the older parts were wearing away. It was a big job, and all the rabbits had to help. Even us young kittens: we carried baskets of soil out for the diggers and brought them drinks and food.

The soil was soft and loamy, and the new burrow fast appeared. Then, after a few days *of digging, a cry went out that something had been found. I remember dashing down there with my friends, expecting to find pots of gold or fairy treasure. Instead there was something . . . something else.*

It makes my fur crawl to think of it, even now, after all this time.

The thing. It was there, jutting up out of the ground like a great rotten fang. It was dark metal: iron of some sort, perhaps. We had seen lumps of iron before. We knew it was metal the Goddess hated, and that no rabbit could work it. But they had been tiny lumps – the size of your paw or so. This thing was huge. As tall as the biggest rabbit in the warren, and then some.

And there was something about it. It didn't feel right. You could sense it pulsing and grinding inside itself – as if it were angry or full of something nasty.

It was jagged and rough, but under the surface you could see things. Things that seemed to twitch and move. Spikes and horns here, a tentacle there. Even an eye or a mouth.

We all knew it was evil. That was very clear. Nobody wanted to go near the new longburrow after that. Our priestess sealed off the tunnel with magic charms, and we all tried to pretend it hadn't happened, but none of us slept easy after that night.

And then the noises started.

Deep in the dead of night, you could hear them. Voices mostly. Some belonging to rabbits, some belonging to something else. Sometimes there was laughing and chanting too, although not in any language we had heard before. And then the hammering started.

From that day Crama, our chieftain, was almost never seen in daylight.

Every night, when the warren was asleep, he went down there with his soldiers to be near that thing. It changed them. Told them how to take the iron and hammer it and shape it. Whispered dark secrets and forbidden promises in their ears. That evil

*shard of metal took our chief, it did. What
could it have offered him? Power, strength,
riches? Maybe it took away all his caution
and gave him something else instead?*

*I know this for sure, though: all the time
he was forging it into something else, it was
forging him as well.*

The bard stopped a moment – he could see the
little rabbits enraptured. The older rabbits too. The
entire longburrow was now hanging on his every
word. He cleared his throat and continued.

*A week or so later, the night hammering
stopped.*

*The next day, Crama showed himself. It
was a Mer's Day feast, as I remember – the
day we honoured our goddess of the sea.
We were all sat in the longburrow, about to
start a dinner of grilled mackerel and crab
cakes. The last fish I ever ate.*

*Crama walked into the longburrow with his
soldiers, and every rabbit almost screamed.*

The oversized Copperpot wasn't on his head any more. In its place was a different helmet. An iron one, all twisted and spiked. It had two horns, like a mockery of the Goddess's helm, but they were mismatched and jagged things. He walked taller and broader than before. This was not Crama the Cautious any more. This was a part of that evil iron thing, walking around in rabbit form.

He spoke to us then, in a grating, scraping voice that none of us recognised. In the years since, I've tried to remember what he said, but the truth is I wasn't really listening. All I could do at the time was stare. Stare at that iron war-helm of his, but mostly at his eyes – his and all his soldiers'. They weren't rabbit eyes any more, you see. They were red like rusted iron or dried blood.

Some rabbits stood up and protested. Our priestess was one, my uncle another. The soldiers grabbed them and took them away, deep into the warren. We never saw them again.

That night, my family and I (and a lot of

others besides) all crept out of Sandywell
and ran. We ran for our lives, and we
didn't stop until we had forests, rivers and
mountains in between that place and us. If
you're listening to this, and you want to stay
safe and free, you'll do the same.

And wherever you end up, take this one
piece of advice from an old rabbit who's kept
her skin long enough to know: keep your
warren safe, keep your warren warm but . . .
don't dig too deep.

The bard folds up the old leather parchment and
tucks it back inside his belt pouch. There is silence
for a little while afterwards, as the little rabbits
imagine horrid things buried in the earth beneath
their bottoms. But buried is perhaps better than a
wandering witch putting curses on you and turning
you into a monster. The bard looks at the little girl
rabbit and sees she is slightly less terrified, which
will have to do.

The silence doesn't last for long, of course.

'Was the Copperpot a magic weapon like Starclaw

then? Did the chief turn into Scramashank?' A little speckled rabbit looks up at the bard with huge saucer eyes glinting in the firelight. Her friends all nod, wanting to find out too.

'Even more questions? You are an inquisitive one indeed, aren't you?' The bard reaches down and tweaks one of her floppy ears. 'Way back, before memories even began, the Goddess herself gave each of the twelve rabbit tribes a magic treasure. Sandywell had the Copperpot, and Starclaw was the prize of Munbury warren, who were once the greatest tribe of all.'

'Did we get a gift? Where's our magic weapon?'

The bard laughs at this and winks over at Chief Hubert, who is rolling his eyes as he sips at a bowl of buttery turnip soup. 'Thornwood warren is too new for that. It hasn't been here much more than sixty years. In fact, at the time of my story, it was little more than a scrape in the ground – which is why the Gorm never bothered with it.'

'Where are the magic gifts now then? Who's got the dagger? Did the Gorm destroy the helmet? What other magic things were there?'

'Yes, yes!' call the other rabbits. 'Where is the dagger now? What happened to it? What happened?'

Bang! The bard brings his wooden flagon down on the tabletop, making all the little rabbits jump.

They squeak and shiver for a bit, until he fixes them all with his best glare. Then they are completely silent. When all that can be heard is the crackle of the fire and the slurping of Chief Hubert's soup, he speaks again.

'I do believe we had a deal, didn't we?'

'They were running from the Gorm!' one rabbit calls out.

'Podkin had just toppled a tree on to the riders!' yells another.

'They were squished like raspberry jam! There was blood everywhere! And eyeballs and things!'

'All right, all right,' says the bard. 'That's quite enough gory detail. Now. Let me carry on where I left off . . .'

CHAPTER FIVE

Redwater

Well. As you so beautifully described, the fleeing rabbits had just toppled a tree on to two Gorm riders. Very impressive too.

After they had stood for a few moments, taking in what had happened, slowly realising they were still alive, they headed off into the woods again.

The sun was well risen now, and they followed it eastward, crunching through the snow as drips from melting icicles pattered on their heads and ran down their necks, making them shiver even more.

Before long they stumbled down another bank

and on to a narrow, frozen river. Paz, who actually *had* been paying attention in those geography lessons, recognised it as the Red River.

'This is the river that runs past Redwater warren! Don't you remember it?'

Podkin was too cold to remember anything, even if he had been listening, about river names and types of trees. The terror of nearly being caught, and the amazement at the power of Starclaw was gone. All he really wanted to do now was lay down in the soft white snow and fall asleep forever. But there was a dim little thought tugging away at the corner of his mind. Hadn't they used to come here at Midsummer, every other year? There had been other little rabbits, hadn't there? And dandelion salad, with carrot juice dressing. He was sure he remembered that.

'W-was it different then? Not w-w-white everywhere?'

Paz gave him a worried look and grabbed him by the arm. They half-ran, half-fell all the way along the riverbank until they came to an arched wooden bridge, and from there they followed a snowy track, cut into the forest floor. It led them to a pair of oak

doors, set into the hillside. Notched Ogham writing, carved into the gateposts, declared it to be Redwater.

'Thank the Goddess,' said Paz, tears in her eyes as she used the last of her strength to bang on the door. Podkin could do nothing but stand and shiver at her side, and little Pook was too cold even for that.

After a few moments, the warren door creaked open, and a ginger-furred guard-rabbit poked out his head.

Now, Paz and Podkin might have been half-frozen, but they had been here several times before, and they remembered the famous hospitality of the Redwater rabbits. Everyone for miles around knew how excitable and fun-loving they were. Any rabbit who stopped here was practically dragged inside and made to eat, sing and dance until they dropped.

Which is why they were shocked by this gloomy-faced, dreary soldier who peered at them now. His ears drooped, his eyes were shadowed and bloodshot. His leather armour was unlaced, unpolished, battered and torn. It barely fitted, hanging off him like old clothes on a scarecrow. If they hadn't been so frozen, they might have wondered why such a skinny, undersized rabbit was doing the job of a hardened warrior.

'What d'you want?' he said, not looking like he cared in the slightest.

Paz could sense something was wrong but was too desperate to listen to her gut. She cleared her throat and spoke. 'We need help. Please.'

'The G-g-gorm are after us,' Pod added.

'S-soop?' whispered Pook, poking a shivering nose out of Paz's tunic.

'We're from Munbury warren,' said Paz. 'We're Chief Lopkin's children.'

The guard's eyes widened at this, and he slammed the door on them. For an awful moment, Podkin and Paz thought they were being shut out, but then they heard the guard shouting for help through the doors.

'Are they g-g-going to let us in?' Podkin asked, through chattering teeth.

'I think so,' said Paz. 'But something's up. We'd better hide the dagger.'

Podkin just looked at it dumbly, as if he was wondering how the thing had appeared in his hand. Quickly, Paz snatched it off him, wrapped it around with the cloth and shoved it inside her tunic, next to Pook, who gave a weak little squeak of protest. She had just hidden it away when the door creaked open again, this time revealing a familiar face: Lady Russet, the Redwater chieftain's wife.

Even though Podkin's brain was practically an ice cube, he could see the terrible difference in the Lady. Before, she had been a plump, bristling bundle of life, with zinging fur, a bubbling giggle and eyes that sparked like glimmers of summer sunlight.

Now, her skin hung off her face in folds. Lines of worry creased her brow; her eyes were hollow, haunted and red-rimmed, as if she'd been crying. Crying for a long, long time. When she spoke, her voice was light and happy, but it sounded forced, as if she was trying to hide some great sadness.

'Why, if it isn't little Paz and Podkin! How you've grown since the summer. And is that tiny Pook nestled there? You poor things – you look frozen half to death! Is it true what my guard says about the Gorm? In Munbury warren? Come in, come in at once! You'll be safe here, I promise.'

Podkin knew this wasn't right: that he should

probably turn and run back into the icy woods, but he could hear the crackle of a fire somewhere down inside the warren; and he could smell roasting parsnips and freshly baked bread. At that moment, getting warm and eating were more important to him than anything else, even his safety. That might sound silly to *you*, sitting by a toasty hearthside with a belly full of turnip soup, but try spending the night running for your life through a Midwinter forest You'd chew the legs off a rabid badger for a snack and somewhere cosy to sleep.

In fact, warmth and food *were* more important than anything else right then. Although the little rabbits didn't know it, they were actually very close to freezing to death. If Podkin had lain down in that snowdrift like he'd wanted to, the sleep he drifted off in would have been his last. He would have woken up in the Land Beyond, and there is no coming back from that place.

So that was how they came to enter Redwater warren, even though it was a mistake Podkin would regret for the rest of his life . . .

They were led through to the longburrow and sat down on benches next to the fire. Lady Redwater went off 'to see that rooms were made ready for them', and some silent, shuffling serving rabbits brought out hot buttered parsnips and a few small loaves of bread.

As soon as the blood started moving round his body again, Podkin's hands began to shake so badly he could hardly hold his plate. He managed a bite of parsnip eventually, and it burnt and tingled as it slipped down his throat. It was the best feeling he had ever had.

After a little while, the shaking stopped, and he found himself gulping down mouthfuls and tearing through the bread like a starved rabbit. Paz was doing the same, and little Pook even began to move around a bit. His nose wrinkled and his big eyes peered out from Paz's tunic. 'Neeps! Neeps!' he called, opening his mouth like a baby bird, as Paz spooned hot parsnips inside.

As his body thawed out, so did Podkin's wits. He noticed the longburrow was dark and damp. Thick cobwebs filled the corners, and the fire before them was a tiny one, nestled amongst huge banks of ash. The fireplace hadn't been swept for months.

He looked around at the tables and benches,

remembering the feast days of Midsummer, when the hall had been packed to the rafters with cheery rabbits. There was hardly any furniture left now. And those chairs – had they been patched up? Was the back of that bench splintered?

The food wasn't quite right, either. The parsnips were stringy, the bread gritty and burnt on the outside. The last feast day they had eaten a huge glorious meal here. There had been a giant carrot, hollowed out so that when it was cut, a cascade of roasted turnips and swedes tumbled over the table. Now *that* was proper Redwater food. Not this hastily cobbled-together meal in front of them.

Once he'd started noticing one or two little things, his eyes picked out more. Were those gouge-marks on the earth wall there? What were those dried red stains, spattered on the floor?

And also, come to think of it: where were the children? The chieftain's children they had played hide-and-seek and blind bunny's bluff with every year since he could walk? They were as noisy, loud and bubbly as any Redwater rabbit ever was. If they weren't in the longburrow itself, they should at least be able to hear them shouting and chasing each other somewhere in the warren. This was Bramblemas morning, after all. There should have been a cluster of little rabbits in the longburrow, all showing off what the Midwinter Rabbit had brought them in the night. At least, that was always what happened in Munbury warren.

I had been hoping for a set of wooden soldiers, Podkin thought. He wondered if they had been delivered anyway and were sitting next to his empty bed, or whether the Midwinter Rabbit knew about the Gorm and had kept away. It didn't seem important any more, even though it had been all he'd thought about for weeks. *How quickly your life can turn upside down.*

'Paz,' he whispered. 'Where d'you think Rufus and Rusty are? Wouldn't they have come out to see us if they knew we were here?'

Paz nodded. Her eyes had been zipping everywhere, noticing the same things as Podkin. Mostly, she had been staring at a metal sculpture that she hadn't seen before. A tall iron pedestal that jutted up from the longburrow floor. It wasn't a model of anything in particular, just a mass of twists and coils, all jagged, uneven and unfinished. *Why do they have an iron statue in their warren?* she wondered. Everyone knew that kind of metal was hated by the Goddess. And what was it about the thing that set her fur on edge? It reminded her of something, but her poor, frozen, terrified mind couldn't quite place it.

And then it came to her.

The Gorm.

She wanted to tell Podkin but didn't speak because two serving rabbits had just entered the room. They were carrying some kind of large box between them, covered over with a thick blanket. They kept to the shadows as they edged their way around the longburrow. They had their heads down, but Paz could see them darting nervous, scared glances at them as they passed. Out through the hallway to the main doors they went. When they were gone, she hissed at Pod. 'What was that they were carrying?'

Pod was about to shrug when he heard a muffled cawing sound coming from the hallway. Some kind of animal? A bird? That sound – they had heard it before, just a few short hours ago. Podkin and Paz looked at each other, both thinking the same thought at the same time.

It's not a box, but a cage. And inside must be one of the Gorm's spy birds. A warped, tortured crow with dead eyes and rusted metal feathers. The bird, the statue, the dead, empty warren. Suddenly it all made terrible sense.

'They're working for the Gorm!' Podkin hissed. 'They're letting them know we're here!'

The Gorm must have taken Redwater, just like they had Munbury. Chief Russet must have been killed, his guards murdered, and the rest of the warren turned into slaves. And as for the children . . . Podkin didn't like to think. Without its heart and soul, the warren was slowly dying. They had chosen the worst possible place to run to.

'We have to get out!' Paz started to say, but Podkin was already up and running. She grabbed Pook and went to follow when, from the corner of her eye, she caught sight of the iron pillar. Something inside it had squirmed, juddered, like a fat eel stuck in a shallow puddle of mud. Could that even be possible? And then it made a sound: a grinding, screeching wail that grew louder and louder.

She didn't stop to hear any more. Clutching Pook, she dashed after her brother as fast as her quick rabbit legs would carry her. They sprinted out of the longburrow, in the opposite direction of the main entrance, just as a shout went up from the gallery above. Someone had been up there watching them, and from the voice it sounded a lot like Lady Russet herself.

'Stop them! Don't let them escape!'

Into the tunnels of the warren they ran, the screams echoing behind them. Heading away from the main doors may have seemed a daft thing to do, but Podkin knew there would be guards there. He also knew warrens had many little back entrances and boltholes. He could hear his father's voice reciting one of his favourite phrases: *'a warren with only one entrance is basically a trap.'* A trap – like the one they had just walked into.

They dashed through dark winding corridors, changing direction every time they heard footsteps nearby. The Redwater rabbits were closing in on them, hounding them through the tunnels like ferrets used to chase their small fluffy ancestors.

Shouting voices echoed behind them, and little Pook began to wail as he was bounced around inside Paz's tunic. 'Neeps! Neeps!' He could sense his sister's fear but was also very concerned that his meal had been interrupted.

'There!' Paz shouted. 'Up ahead!'

The tunnel had become lighter, and as they rounded a corner, they saw a small open gateway and the snowy forest beyond. They sprinted for it, as fast as terrified rabbits can, as Lady Russet's voice called out behind them: 'Seal the warren! Close all the gates!'

Slams and bangs began to echo through the passageways and, with numb horror, Podkin saw a metal portcullis begin to grind downwards over the doorway ahead. Their escape was being blocked. They were going to be trapped inside.

Sometimes, when your life is in real danger, when everything seems lost, there is a well of energy deep within you that can give you a final, desperate surge of power. It isn't always much: but often it's just enough to scrape through trouble by a whisker.

Podkin and Paz reached for theirs now, and doubled their speed down the tunnel, as the heavy grille clanked further and further down.

Paz reached it first, and dropped to her knees, sliding underneath the portcullis's prongs and out into the snow. Podkin was a split second behind. He copied his sister, kicking his legs out and falling backwards to skid underneath. Looking up, he saw the roof of the tunnel pass by: the gateway, the falling portcullis, and then the grey sky of the open air above.

I did it! he thought. *I'm free!* But then there came a sharp searing pain in his ear. He tried to get up, but something was holding his head down. Something very painful. He heard Paz scream, and he twisted around to see what had happened.

The portcullis was down, and they were on the outside: or at least most of them was. One of his long silky brown ears was still inside, and speared through it – holding him in place – was a prong of the portcullis.

He had been pinned to the ground.

He was trapped.

CHAPTER SIX

One-Ear

P az heard the clang of the portcullis behind her
and turned to see Podkin lying safely outside
the warren. She felt a surge of relief, which quickly
disappeared when she saw the look of agony on
his face.

Why isn't he getting up? she thought. *Has he
sprained an ankle? Hurt his back?* And then she saw
the portcullis prong, spearing his ear to the ground.
That was when she screamed.

She dashed to his side and took his hand. 'Oh,
Pod! Your ear!'

Her brother's eyes were bulging and his teeth were gnashing in pain. She realised he must be trying his hardest not to scream, so that the Redwater rabbits wouldn't discover where they'd gone. The poor thing could hardly move his head. There was no way they could escape into the woods now.

A voice came from back in the tunnel, somewhere in the dark. 'If only you hadn't run. Then none of this would have happened.'

As Paz watched, she saw a figure step towards the portcullis, closer to the light. It was Lady Russet. The gaunt, haunted Lady Russet, with cold dead eyes.

'Let us go, milady,' Paz looked up at her and pleaded. 'You were always our friend. Don't let the Gorm take us!'

'The living statue they left here has sensed you. We have already sent the crow,' said Lady Russet. 'By now it has reached its masters and is calling them to us. It is too late.'

'How can you do this? Why would you help them? They're evil, Lady Russet. They killed our father!'

For a moment, there was something like pity in the Lady's eyes. Paz thought she even saw a tear form there, before it trickled away into her fur. 'They killed my husband too,' she said, her voice little more than a whisper. 'And all our guards and warriors. But they have my children ... Rufus and Rusty. If I give you to them, I might get them back.'

Paz's fury at this cowardly, spineless thing the chieftain's wife had become suddenly overflowed. She jumped up and grabbed the bars of the portcullis, shouting down the tunnel at her. 'What would my father say if he saw you now? What would your *husband* say? Call yourself a rabbit? You're no better than a weasel, you ... you ... *traitor*!'

Lady Russet jumped backwards, eyes wide, vanishing into the shadows. It was a good few moments before she spoke again, and when she did her voice was shaky and broken, as if she were holding back from sobbing.

'It won't be long until they are here. Your brother is stuck, and I won't free him, but if you are gone when they arrive, I will say he came here on his own. You and the little one can escape. That's the best I can do.'

With that, she was gone, back into the warren,

leaving the little rabbits cold and frightened in the snow.

*

'You heard her, Paz,' said Podkin eventually. 'You have a chance to get away. Leave me here, and take Pook somewhere safe.'

Paz gritted her teeth and shook the portcullis bars. 'I am *not* leaving you behind,' she said. 'There must be some way to get you free.'

'Caw! Caw!' Pook was wiggling around inside her tunic, shouting at the top of his voice.

'What?' Paz snapped at him. 'The crow's gone, Pook.'

'Caw! Caw!'

'It's gone, Pook! No bird! Gone! Now stop shouting at me so I can think of what to do!'

The baby rabbit gave a frustrated yell, then started wriggling about like mad, pushing the cloth-wrapped dagger out of Paz's robes where she had stowed it. It took a moment for her to realise what he was doing.

'Of course! Not *caw*, but *claw*! Starclaw! You're a genius, Pook.' Paz gave him a quick nuzzle, then dragged Starclaw out, ripping off the cloth covering as fast as she could.

Clang! She swung it hard against the portcullis. She tried again and again, but nothing happened. *Clang! Clang!*

'Aaargh ...' Podkin moaned. The vibrations were like tiny explosions in his wounded ear. 'Stop doing that!'

'Oh, whiskers! The gate's iron. The stupid dagger won't cut through it. How did they even get an iron gate? Unless the Gorm gave it to them ...' Paz cursed again and shoved the dagger into the snow. What was the point of having a magic weapon if you couldn't use it half the time?

Podkin whimpered, his hands reaching up to his pinned ear. There must be some way to free him. Could she cut away the stone of the gateway floor? Or the lintel above, perhaps? She wondered how much time they had.

Her question was answered by a horn blast, somewhere on the other side of the warren. They had hardly any time at all.

'Go,' Podkin said again. 'Just go.'

No. Paz shook her head. There had to be some other way around it. Her quick little mind whirred, ticking through all the possibilities. In the end there was only one option.

'Pod.' She gripped him by the hand and squeezed. 'The dagger can't cut through iron, but it can cut through ... your ear.'

Paz gulped. Podkin gulped.

The portcullis had speared his ear over halfway down. He would have to lose nearly the whole thing.

'Please don't,' he said. 'Just leave me for the Gorm. They probably won't kill me. Will they?'

'You're officially the chieftain of Munbury warren now,' said Paz. 'They'll do to you what they did to Father. Scramashank will wear your skull on his belt.'

'But my *ear.*'

'I have to do it now, Pod. There isn't much time.'

Podkin and Paz looked at each other. Finally Podkin nodded.

Paz pulled the dagger out of the snow. Inside her tunic, Pook squeaked and hid his eyes.

'Hang on,' said Paz. She remembered a lesson on

wood lore about how spider webs could help stop a wound bleeding. She stood on tiptoe and pulled a good handful of matted cobwebs from around the door, ignoring the fat spiders that scuttled over her fingers, angry at having their winter sleep broken. Then she lowered the dagger tip to rest against Pod's ear.

'Will it hurt?' he said.

'It might.' Paz remembered the way the dagger had chopped through the tree trunk like it was butter. 'But it'll be quick.'

'Then do it,' said Podkin, closing his eyes.

It was funny how he didn't feel anything at first. Not the slice, not the cobwebs being pressed over the wound, nor the handfuls of snow after that. It was funny to be running off into the woods, leaving a part of his body behind. But the funniest thing of all was that, even after his ear had been sliced off, he could still feel the burning pain of the portcullis piercing it. A burning pain in an ear that was no longer there.

INTERLUDE

'Hey! That wasn't how he lost his ear!'

'It was clawed off by a wildcat!'

'No! A vampire rabbit ate it in one bite!'

'It was pulled off by a giant lop!'

'I heard he chopped it off himself, and made it into a boat to escape an island full of monsters!'

The bard folds his arms and gives the little rabbits his best glare. Eventually their squeaking subsides, and they sit frowning up at him in silence.

'Roasted radishes, you are a noisy bunch! I don't really care what you've heard about how Podkin became the One-Eared,' he says. 'This is *my* story. It belongs to me. And in my story, he had to cut it off to escape the Gorm.'

'That's daft,' says the inquisitive rabbit. 'How can

anyone own a story? It isn't a real thing. It's just words.'

'Stories belong to the teller,' says the bard. 'At least half of them do. The other part belongs to the listeners. When a good story is told to a good listener, the pair of them own it together.'

'So the story is ours now?' asks another rabbit.

'It will be,' says the bard, 'if I ever get to finish the blooming thing.'

'I think it makes sense,' says a quiet piebald rabbit at the front. 'There's no such thing as vampire rabbits anyway. I always thought he lost his ear in a battle, but this version sounds like something that would have happened.'

'Thank you,' says the bard. 'You're obviously a very sensible little rabbit. The chieftain's son, also, might I guess?'

Behind him, Chief Hubert swells with pride (or he would do, if he wasn't already as swollen as any rabbit could get without exploding all over the longburrow). The inquisitive rabbit makes the most of the interruption to pipe up once more.

'But *how* do you know what happened? If you weren't really there, I mean.'

The bard sighs and rolls his eyes. 'I'm a storyteller. I tell stories. That's my job.'

'So this *is* just made up then.' The inquisitive rabbit doesn't look very impressed. 'Well, if you're going to make up a story anyway, you might as well put vampire rabbits in. Vampire rabbits are exciting.'

'By the Goddess's sacred celery ...' The bard puts his head in his hands and makes a quiet sobbing sound.

The sensible rabbit digs his friend in the ribs with an elbow. 'Vampire rabbits aren't *real*,' he says. 'If the story has things in it that don't seem real, then we won't want to believe it. If we don't want to believe it, the story falls apart. Then there really is no point in listening to it.'

The bard peeps out between his fingers and gives the sensible rabbit a wink.

'There is a god,' he says, 'of bards and storytellers. His name is Clarion, and he has been known to whisper the art of stories into the ears of a chosen few rabbits while they sleep. I believe he must have paid you a visit or two, my wise little friend.'

It is the sensible rabbit's turn to puff up with pride, making him look like a tiny replica of his father. A hint of what will he become when it is his turn to become chieftain.

'Very well.' The bard clears his throat and gives his audience another glare. 'If you've quite finished interrupting, might I be allowed to continue the story?'

CHAPTER SEVEN

The Witch in the Woods

I t was very hard for the little rabbits to go back out into the winter forest. What little warmth they had gained from Redwater warren soon vanished, and this time they had no idea where to run. As far as they knew, the whole world was against them and nowhere was safe.

They knew they didn't have much of a head start, either. The Gorm would be arriving at Redwater soon, and in five short minutes they would discover Podkin's severed ear. After that, they simply had to stroll along the trail of footprints in the snow, and then it would all be over in the flash of a twisted iron blade.

Podkin wasn't too worried by it all. He had lost quite a lot of blood, which tended to make you dizzy and dozy. He was currently dreaming that he was walking on top of a fluffy white cloud. His sister was there, carrying a talking carrot that looked a lot like his brother, Pook; and for some reason, his ear was very sore. He thought he'd probably wake up soon, then go out and see if he could find a nice spot by the river for a snooze.

Paz dragged him along by the arm, casting worried glances at his missing ear. The wound was still oozing blood, and the fur on his head was thickly matted with it. She needed to stop and bind it, but there wasn't time.

Pook had also started shivering again. He was making quiet, miserable little whines, and she wasn't sure how much more of the cold he could take. She was trying her hardest to move quickly, not to leave such obvious tracks, to keep to the deeper parts of the wood ...

All in all, she had begun to think it might be

better if the Gorm did get them. At least it would all be over quickly.

Which is why she wasn't too surprised when they stepped into a clearing and saw a hunched, twisted crow sitting on a tree stump and staring at them with blank red eyes.

'Oh no,' she moaned. 'Oh no.'

The crow blinked and tilted its spiked metal head. Its beak opened slightly, dripping some oily, coppery fluid. Its feathers rattled and scraped against each other, giving off a cloud of powdery orange rust. Paz tried to think of some way to stop it before it flew off and betrayed their whereabouts. Throw the dagger at it? Jump on top of the thing and squash it? There was really nothing she could do.

'Caaa!' it squawked, and began to spread its wings for take-off, when suddenly it exploded with a clang and a puff of iron feathers. Paz shrieked and stared at the drifting cloud of jagged plumage. The crow itself had been knocked to the floor, stone dead.

'I hate those pesky birds,' said someone on the other side of the clearing. Paz raised the dagger, ready to defend herself, as a stooped old she-rabbit in a patched cloak crunched towards them through the snow. Her hand clutched a leather sling, empty now of its pebble bullet. 'They should learn to mind their own beeswax.'

'Um ... hello?' said Paz.

'Is it morning yet, Mummy?' said Podkin.

'Soop?' said Pook.

'It's about time you three showed up,' the she-rabbit said. 'I've been waiting about in the snow for ages. Blooming cold, my poor feet are.'

'You've ... you've been expecting us?' Now Paz wasn't sure if *she* was dreaming. Or was this another agent of the Gorm? She didn't have any metal shards poking out of her face, but still ...

'Expecting you, dear? I should say so. Saw it in the bones, years ago. And now we'd better hurry and see to that ear. We'll lose him if we don't, and then we'll lose everything else.'

Paz looked at her poor suffering brother and then stared at the old rabbit, trying to work out whether to trust her or not. She was clearly mad, but was she a safer bet than trying to escape the Gorm on their own? The she-rabbit stared back, with piercing blue eyes that looked much younger than her face. Her nose wrinkled and twitched as she waited for Paz to make her decision. Finally, she nodded.

'All right. We'll come with you.' *But if you try to trick us ...* Paz had Starclaw clutched in one hand. It would cut through the rabbit's flesh just like it had Podkin's ear.

The she-rabbit nodded, as if satisfied that things were going to plan. 'Good, good. Just what you're supposed to say, dear.' She walked to the edge of the clearing, and then paused to draw a bronze sickle from her belt. Bending down, she started cutting a slender pine sapling with it. While she was busy, a thousand thoughts raced through Paz's mind. *What if she's a traitor like Lady Russet? What if she's a witch? Don't you remember what happens to little rabbits that go off with witches in the forest?*

The she-rabbit finished cutting off the sapling and used it like a broom to swish away their footprints in the snow. When she had finished, she looked up, an impatient frown on her face.

'Well? Are you coming or not?' she said. 'Hop along, my little bunnies.'

Then she turned and vanished into the undergrowth.

*

Witch or not, there wasn't much else Paz could do but follow. They wound their way through the bushes and trees, Podkin moaning softly and stopping every now and then for the she-rabbit to hide their tracks, until they came to the biggest oak tree that Paz had ever seen. It had a cascade of gnarled, squirming roots that spilled down from a sloped bank of earth. The towering trunk was thick enough to be four or five centuries old, and its branches – weighed down with snow – dipped to the forest floor, making a kind of latticework cave. A cage of wood and snow that, in a happier time, would have made an amazing play den.

However, it wouldn't be much good at keeping out the Gorm. Paz watched as the she-rabbit ducked through the branches, hoping she had a better plan than just hiding amongst the tangles of roots.

Instead, she pushed at a spot on the packed earth of the bank. It looked like a bare patch of mud, covered in moss, lichen and dead leaves but – to Paz's surprise – it swung open to reveal a hidden door. She hurried inside, helping the bleary Podkin along. As soon as they were in, the old rabbit shut the door and bolted it.

This is it, thought Paz. *This is when the witch makes us into a pie, or maybe some kind of casserole.*

But no such thing happened. Instead, the she-rabbit hung up her cloak and busied herself by stoking the fire inside a little clay stove. She put a pot on top and poured in water from a clay pitcher, before taking Podkin's hand and leading him to sit on a little stool by the hearth.

Paz couldn't help worrying that the warming stove might be intended for them but, seeing as they weren't being eaten *just* yet, she took the chance to look around. They were in a tidy little house, burrowed beneath the huge roots of the oak. The earth between them had been whitewashed, and reed mats covered the floor. Pots, pans and utensils hung from the ceiling, and there was a small fireplace, complete with mantelpiece, where the stove nestled.

Shelves had been carved into the earth of the walls, and more had been added, made from old warped planks of wood. Every inch of these were packed with a strange collection of items, too many for Paz to really take in.

She saw lots of clay pots and jars, all labelled with neat Ogham writing, some overflowing with dried herbs and bulbs: wild garlic, rosemary, foxglove, rosehip and lots of mushrooms, like ink cap, blusher, penny bun, brittlegill and angel's bonnet.

Paz saw many other, stranger things that she could only wonder about. A glass jar filled with bird skulls; a painted wooden mask with fangs and huge eyes; a clay model of a peaceful rabbit, sitting cross-legged, from whose head a spiral of scented smoke slowly uncurled.

So this is what a witch has in her house, she thought. But there were other, more homely things too: a bed in the corner, a spinning wheel, loom and some cupboards. There was even a leaded-glass window, framed by tree roots. Paz went over and peered outside. What she saw made her clap her hands over her mouth to stop her from screaming.

A pack of Gorm riders were a few metres away, grinding their way through the snow. Their hunched iron beasts were ploughing up the ground, spattering it with black oil, while their riders sat atop, slowly turning their heads this way and that. Their jagged, serrated swords twitched, hungry for rabbit flesh. She could hear the screeching and grating of metal; she could smell the hot oil and burnt-blood stink. Any moment now, they would spot the secret door in the bank and come crashing through . . .

'Don't you worry about them,' said the she-rabbit, as she took the water from the stove and set it down beside Podkin. 'They won't find us here. There's enough glamours and 'chantments about this place that Hern himself couldn't find it, if I didn't want him to.'

And true enough, now the Gorm were turning their mounts and seemed to be heading off towards the far end of the bank and away.

Proper magic. A little voice in Paz's head said. *Not only a witch, but a good one.* She smiled to herself and went over to where Podkin was sitting.

'This is nasty,' said the she-rabbit. 'Going to need stitches.' She had a blunt, matter-of-fact way about her that Paz found reassuring somehow. She clearly knew what she was doing.

'Will he be all right?' Paz asked.

'As right as a one-eared rabbit can be. Still, it'll do him a favour in the long run. Nobody'd be as interested in telling stories about a normal rabbit.'

Stories? The long run? What was she talking about?

As Paz watched, the old rabbit gave Podkin something to drink that sent him to sleep. They moved him over to the bed, and then cleaned the wound with warm water. The she-rabbit stitched it with a bone needle and thread, before putting on a poultice and binding it tight. She spoke as she worked, and Paz discovered her name was Brigid, and that she lived in the woods alone, foraging for food, herbs and anything else she needed. She didn't say, but Paz guessed she had been living under the oak tree for a long time. Long enough to lose the knack of talking to others. Social skills were very important for warren rabbits, but Paz guessed you didn't need them when the only person you had to worry about pleasing was yourself.

As soon as Podkin was quietly sleeping, Brigid made some stinging-nettle broth, which Pook gulped down. They sat by the fire, listening to the sounds of the crackling wood. It felt wonderful to be warm, fed and safe, even though their enemies were still not so very far away.

Paz found herself drifting off to sleep. Pook was already snoring on the hearthrug, and at some point Paz joined him, dimly aware of Brigid covering them both with a patchwork blanket. She tried to say 'thank you', or to ask one of the many questions that were whizzing about her head, but the sleepiness was too strong. She let herself fall into it.

*

When she awoke, she saw Brigid sitting on a chair by the stove, holding the magic dagger Starclaw in her hands. She was turning it over, thoughtfully, pausing every now and then to peer at the copper face on the hilt.

Paz watched her, wondering what to say. She didn't want to appear rude, but seeing Brigid with the dagger made her uneasy: partly because she didn't think she should be touching it, and also because there was a good chance it might slice off her fingers.

The old rabbit didn't even look at Paz, but somehow still knew she was awake. 'Powerful magic in this here dagger,' she said. 'One of the Twelve Gifts of the Goddess, if I'm not mistaken.'

'How ...' Paz began, not knowing whether to admit what Starclaw was. 'How d'you know that?'

'Got one myself.' Brigid smiled and pulled the little copper sickle from her belt. When she brought it near the dagger, it flashed blue for an instant. Paz thought she saw Starclaw give an answering twinkle.

'How did you get one?' Paz asked. 'I thought they were only given to chieftains of the twelve tribes?'

'They were.' Brigid tucked the sickle away again and looked into the flickering flames of the stove. 'I was a princess once. Not that you'd know it now, of course. I reckon you must be too. My father was the chief of Redwater warren, a long time back now. One of his Guard double-crossed him and forced him out. All our family had to leave, cast out of our home like wandering tinkers. I knew about the sickle and decided *that* lot didn't deserve to have it, so I took it with me. It glows red whenever it's near poison. Blue when it's near something good. Taught me all I know about herb-craft and healing, it did.'

Paz found it hard to imagine the bent old

she-rabbit as a princess, sitting at the head table in the longburrow, or dressed in her finest for the Carrotmas feast at harvest time. 'Was it Chief Russet who did that to your family? He always seemed such a friendly rabbit . . .'

'Not him, but his father before, the evil two-faced son of a weasel. He was the captain of the Honour Guard as well. Always too trusting, my old father. And look where it got him. My folks moved on afterwards, but I stayed here in the woods. I watched them turn the warren inside out, looking for my sickle. And it was here with me the whole time.' She gave a dry chuckle that sounded like a pile of leaves rustling. When she laughed, Paz could see the little girl still inside her, and she found herself smiling too.

*

The three little rabbits stayed with Brigid for more than two weeks. Podkin slowly began to build up strength while his ear healed. He was very bad-tempered about the whole thing (he used to secretly think his ears were his best feature), but when Brigid told him he had to get as much rest as possible, he was quite pleased. It was the first time in his life that anyone had actually *ordered* him to have lots of snoozes.

Pook enjoyed rolling around on Brigid's floor, playing with the rattling bones and pebbles she used for scrying the future. He just used to toss them about the hearth, making patterns and piles, but Brigid said he had a gift for soothsaying, all the same. Every now and then, she would walk over and examine the bones he had thrown and mumble some comments like 'yes, he will come in handy' and 'must stock up on that sleep potion then'. Pook would look up at her with big, loving eyes and nod in agreement.

Paz went out foraging with the old rabbit several times, and was beginning to learn a fair bit of forest lore. She learnt which mushrooms were good to eat, and which would make you cough up your innards; how to find a squirrel's stash of winter nuts and which trees had bark that you could chew to stop a fever. She learnt the names of plants like Candlewick, Maypops and Love-in-idleness, and how to prepare and use them as medicine.

Podkin watched all this, and couldn't help but

feel a little jealous. After all, *he* was the one with the magic dagger, wasn't he? Shouldn't he be the one learning about spells and poisons? It all sounded quite exciting, even if it did involve having to listen and remember things.

One day he built up enough courage to ask Brigid if she could tell him about magic. 'What kind?' was all the old rabbit said. Paz looked up from where she was crushing dried seeds with a mortar and pestle and pricked her ears with interest.

'There are different kinds?'

'The good kind. And the bad.'

'What's the bad kind?'

'You've seen that, well enough.'

Podkin knew she was talking about the Gorm. To confirm it, Brigid took down one of the strange tapestries from her wall and handed it to him. It showed a circle made up of two snakes, each one eating the body of the other. One was a scaled sea monster with fins and spines: brutal but impressive. The other was a twisted metal thing, all jagged and sharp.

'The two types of magic,' Brigid said. 'Natural magic and dark, iron magic. The world is made

of the two, but they balance each other out like this –
always eating at each other, neither one ever winning.
Least, that's how it's supposed to be.'

'Why the two?' Podkin asked. 'Why can't
there just be natural magic that doesn't want to
hurt anyone?'

In answer, Brigid went to one of her teetering
shelves and took down a carving. It was of two doe
rabbits, standing arm in arm. Podkin recognised one
from the garland of flowers around her neck, and the
little chicks and birds that peeped out from the folds
of her dress: the Goddess Estra, bringer of all life.

The other rabbit looked much more stern. She clutched a fearsome bow, and her robe was cinched around the middle by a belt made of tiny skulls.

'The twin sisters,' Brigid said, making a strange gesture in the air with her paw. 'Estra and Nixha. Goddesses of life and death.'

Podkin stared at the carving, running his fingers over the worked, polished wood. 'I've heard of the Goddess, of course,' he said. 'And I think I remember learning there was someone who took you to the Land Beyond when you died. But we didn't talk about that much, back at home.'

'Most rabbits in these parts don't.' Brigid shook her head. 'But dying is as much a part of life as living. Down south, in the other lands, there's them that worship only Nixha. Funny bunch they are, my dear. I would tell you to stay clear of them, but . . .'

Podkin sensed that the old rabbit was about to go off on one of her strange ramblings again, so he interrupted with another question. 'What do the goddesses have to do with the Gorm then?'

'Well,' said Brigid, taking the statue back and

setting it carefully on her shelf. 'That there is the story at the beginning of everything.'

'Will you tell it to me? Please?'

Brigid huffed and puffed for a bit – there was nettle soup to make and a pile of acorns to shell for bread – but finally she took Podkin over to the hearth where Pook was busy playing with a heap of bones and pebbles. Paz followed too, and the pair of them sat down at Brigid's feet, as though she was a bard telling a bedtime story.

'Right then, dearies,' said Brigid, when she was comfortable. 'The story of the goddesses at the beginning of things, just how the old priestess at Redwater told it to me when I was a fluffy-eared kit.

'It is said by some that back then the world was a dark and evil place. The whole of it: all lands, all seas, was covered by poisonous, seething metal. An evil, wicked mass of horridness that was all part of one being. Gormalech, he was named, and he had eaten whatever was here before, in his never-ending greed and gluttony.

'So, there hangs our world – floating in space, all

covered with nasty, living iron. And it would have stayed there too, cold and alone for all time, if it hadn't been for the goddesses.

'Sometime, goodness only knows how long ago, the goddesses stumbled upon our world and decided it was the place for them. Perhaps they could see through the swirling poison of Gormalech to what was beneath, perhaps they had known the place as it was before he got control of it. Who knows?

'Anyway, they wanted to stop here, and a good job for us that they did. The only problem was: how to get rid of him that was globbing up the place with his stink and poison and nasty iron evilness?

'First of all, they called to him and asked if he wouldn't mind jiggering off somewhere else. Of course, he says "no, not for all the carrots in my back garden", or something like that.

'The next plan, then, was to challenge him to a contest. Winner takes all, sort of thing.

'Estra, the Goddess, chose a game of dice. Fox Paw, she called it, and she trounced old Gormalech.

'Nixha went next, and challenged the evil creature to a contest of archery and needless to say, he lost. Nobody can fire an arrow like Nixha. She never misses, as we will all find out when she comes for us, at the end of our time.

'Finally, it was Gormalech's turn. He simply wanted a fight and, being several thousand times bigger and meaner than those two dainty does, he bashed and beat them to bits.

'Well, the end result of all the competing was that nobody had really won. None of them was best pleased, but they realised they had reached a stalemate. So they came to an agreement. The goddesses would rule the surface of the world, bringing life (and death) back to it, as it was before. Gormalech would go deep underground, where iron and all the other metals come from anyway, and between them they would share the place.

'They called their agreement "the Balance", and promised each other that they would abide by it. From then until the end of time.

'And that is how the story goes.' Brigid dipped a clay cup into the water bowl that sat by the fire and took a long drink. 'Bless my ears, that's the most I've spoken in decades.'

'So Gormalech is the one creating the Gorm?' Podkin said, his voice almost a whisper. 'Because he wants the world back again, do you think? But that means the Balance is broken, because the Gorm are winning now, aren't they?'

'They are. The Balance is indeed broken, my dear. They've found some way to wriggle out of it. They're growing in power. The old magic of the goddesses is under threat.'

Podkin looked over to where Starclaw and Brigid's sickle lay together on the kitchen bench. 'They wanted our dagger. That's what Scramashank was after when he killed Father. But why?'

Brigid shrugged. 'Spite, maybe. Or something worse. I've heard they want the Twelve Gifts destroyed, so that all knowledge of the gods and goddesses fades forever.' She looked down and noticed Podkin was trembling with fear at the thought. 'Don't worry, little one. Magic is a balance, like I said. If it swings too much one way, just means that sometime soon it's going to swing back the other. That's the rules of the deal, don't forget, and that was a deal that can never be broken.'

Podkin thought on that for a moment, and realised it meant that the Gorm were due some revenge. Even though he was still trembling a bit, he managed a hard little smile. Looking up at his sister, he saw she was smiling too.

*

The children missed their parents terribly, and wished more than anything that they could just go home to find everything back the way it was. But even so, the little house in the woods had started to seem like a safe, happy place.

It was only one day, when Paz noticed Brigid scraping the last of her dried nettle leaves from a pot to make soup, that they realised they had to move on. It wasn't fair for the old rabbit to suddenly have to provide for three hungry mouths.

'But she can find more food,' Podkin said, when Paz mentioned it to him. 'She's got you to help her forage now.'

'Yes, but it's winter. And a hard one too. Have you seen how much soup Pook gets through in a day?'

'But where will we go? Redwater was the only safe place we knew, and look how that turned out.'

Podkin ran his fingers over the stump where his left ear had once been.

Paz gave his arm a squeeze. 'Brigid will know of somewhere,' she said.

*

So they asked the old rabbit that night. As it often was with her, it seemed as though she had been expecting the question.

'There is a place, my dears,' she said, with a sigh. 'Not a nice place, or a safe one, but a place where the Gorm won't think to look for you.'

She told them of a town of runaways and refugees that had sprung up amongst the crumbling tombs of an ancient graveyard. An underground warren at the forest's edge, amongst the bones and teeth of creatures long gone from the world.

'Boneroot, it's called. You'll have to be careful there and keep your wits about you, but I promise you, there won't be anyone turned by the Gorm. Every rabbit in the place has run away from them. All their warrens have been taken or enslaved, or just plain burnt to ash. They hate the Gorm as much as I do, and that's a whole lot of hating.'

There were mercenaries there, she said: soldiers you could hire to work for you. She pointed to the silver bracelet Paz wore, and the gold buckle on Podkin's belt. 'If you trade those precious things, you might get someone to fight on your side. Someone to protect you – maybe take you somewhere safe, off across the Eiskalt mountains, where the Gorm have never been. That's what I'd do, if I was you.'

Podkin listened to all this with a sad dread. The last thing he wanted was to go out into the cold, cruel outside world where bits of you got cut off and lost forever. He kept thinking Brigid would change her mind and ask them to stay ... Maybe if he looked especially scared and miserable? But of course, she didn't. She always seemed to know what was going to happen. If *she* thought they were leaving, that meant there was no getting out of it.

Paz, who had spent more time with the old witch, knew a little of how Brigid could unpick and unravel threads of knowledge from the future. Was going to Boneroot something they had to do? Was it part of Podkin's story that she kept mentioning? But if it was a good thing, then why did she sound so sad? What was going to happen to them there? The worries buzzed around her head, making it spin.

Pook didn't want to leave, either. He clutched a few of Brigid's bone pieces in his paw and tried to catch hold of her cloak whenever she moved near him. Paz could see her keeping away on purpose, but reluctantly, as if it was something she had to do. How hard it must be, to know the events that had to happen for the future to unfurl just the way it should. Especially if some of those events were hard or unhappy ones. Would she be able to let them happen, no matter how much it hurt, just because they had to? Paz didn't think she had that kind of strength. It made her admire the old rabbit even more.

Brigid gave them directions for Boneroot, sketched in charcoal on a piece of bark. As a parting gift, she produced some winter cloaks with hoods, knitted hats and scarfs. They were all exactly the right sizes for each of them, but had been folded and put away for so long, they had to have the dust shaken off. Podkin couldn't work out how she had done it.

She had also made him a cloth scabbard in which he could carry Starclaw, strapped to his back and hidden away. She warned him to guard the dagger well, as it was valuable beyond any treasure, and made him promise that he would never let the Gorm touch it.

Finally, they stood in the snow beneath the old oak tree and said their goodbyes. The little rabbits all hugged Brigid and kissed her wrinkled nose. She had tears in her eyes as she waved them off.

As she glanced back through the trees, Paz thought that she saw the sickle on Brigid's belt give a silver glimmer of goodbye, and Podkin, although he had no idea why, felt his magic dagger grow heavier at his side.

CHAPTER EIGHT

Boneroot

Following Brigid's map, the young rabbits found the Red River again and walked along to where it forked. There was a little bridge made of fallen logs lashed together, which they slipped and slid across, and then they followed the smaller branch south again. Before them lay Grimheart forest, a huge mass of trees that filled the entire horizon. The silver-grey, frosted branches were like an ocean of icy wood; the whole Gorm army could be hidden in there, or a thousand packs of hungry wolves, thirsty for blood. Robbers, bandits, murderers – Podkin's

111

imagination ran through them all, until he found it hard to force his feet towards it.

Luckily, they were only going to skirt the forest itself, heading to the east and keeping to the edge of the woods where the trees were thinnest.

Their breath steamed out in misty halos around their heads, but their cloaks and hats kept them warm. Every crunching step, every twig that snapped under their feet, they expected to see a Gorm crow burst from the trees to call its masters down on them. Their ears (or ear, in Podkin's case) were constantly twitching as they listened for the clank of iron armour or the harsh, jagged sound of Gorm-speak.

But either the Gorm had exhausted their search of the forest or Brigid had laid some special charm on their new cloaks. They passed undisturbed and unseen through the frozen winter trees.

Brigid said the journey would take them at least two days and, following her advice, they stopped for the night, found a big snowdrift and scooped out a little cave inside. Pook thought it was great fun, as they all packed the snow hard to make the walls of their little burrow. He had been too small to enjoy the snow last year, and there had been so little time this winter, what with preparing for Bramblemas, and then ... everything that happened after. Paz and Podkin watched him roll in the powdery snow, tasting ice crystals on his tongue and remembering snowball fights and snow burrows they had made in the winters past. How simple everything was then, and how little they had appreciated it.

Their shelter was finished before darkness drew in. They were quite proud of their work: Podkin even built a little wooden shelf for a beeswax candle. He had great fun chopping a whole tree to pieces in the process, delighting in the way Starclaw swished through the trunk as if it was an over-boiled carrot. He might have reduced half the forest to matchwood if Paz hadn't stopped him.

Supper was a small meal of oatcakes and dried beetroot slices, washed down with melted snow-water. When they curled up to sleep for the night, their den was actually very snug and cosy.

Podkin lay awake, looking out through the tunnel

at the stars in the night sky. He could see the Big Radish, the Rat and the Snake: all constellations his mother had taught him as he sat on her knee, looking up at the night sky. She had been on his mind a lot lately, ever since his ear had begun to heal. Rushing to Redwater and the pain of what happened there had been so awful – only now had he started to realise that they'd no idea of what had happened to her.

He nudged Paz awake with his foot.

'What?' she whispered. 'Is something outside?'

'No. Just the stars.'

'What is it then? I'm trying to sleep.'

'It's Mother,' said Podkin. 'We ran off so fast, we don't know whether she's alive or ...' He was about to say 'killed by the Gorm', but it reminded him too much of that last sight of his father, facing down Scramashank with his sword drawn. He couldn't bring himself to speak the words.

'I don't know,' said Paz. 'I hope she's all right, but it's not like we can go back and check. If we do, the Gorm will take us, just like they did the Redwater children.'

'If she *is* back there,' Podkin continued. 'D'you think she'll be like Lady Russet? D'you think she'll start working for the Gorm?'

Paz started to laugh, but it made Pook stir from where he was snuggled against her, so she put a hand over her mouth. 'Can you imagine Mother doing that?'

At first Podkin was shocked. How could she laugh about it, after everything that had happened? But then he imagined his mother, the mighty Lady of Munbury, bowing down and scraping like a humble servant. It just wouldn't be right. Podkin smiled too, then felt tears suddenly spring to his eyes. His fierce, proud mother. She had once chased the chieftain of Deepdell warren out of the longburrow for being rude to his father. Even the toughest warriors in the Munbury Guard were terrified of her and her steely glare. He gave a silent prayer to the Goddess that she was out there, somewhere, looking up at the stars, just like him.

'What's the point in loving people, Paz, if they only get taken away from you? I know we'll never see Father again. Or Mother, probably. It hurts

115

so much to think of it … I almost wish I'd never had parents.'

Paz was silent for a moment before rolling closer and putting an arm around him. 'It does hurt, Pod. It hurts more than anything in the world. I think it always will. That's just part of our life now. But we have to be strong. That's what Father would have wanted.'

Podkin sighed and snuggled into his big sister. 'I know. I was just saying.'

'Besides. They aren't really gone. They'll always be with us. No matter what the Gorm do, we will remember them. They can't take our memories away, can they?'

'Do you still hear Father's voice sometimes? In your head?' Podkin asked. But Paz had fallen asleep, her quiet snores blending with Pook's in their tiny scooped-out snow burrow.

'I do,' Podkin whispered to himself. And then he buried his head in his arms and cried himself silently to sleep.

*

It was late afternoon on the next day when they arrived at Boneroot. Brigid had told them to look out for carved symbols on the tree trunks. A circle, like the snake picture she had shown them, marked with the Ogham symbols for *b* and *r*.

Pook had been the first to spot one, even though he shouldn't have had any idea what they were talking about. He had pointed to a gnarled willow trunk, shouting and cooing so much that Podkin was worried he would bring the Gorm down on them. When they finally got him to be quiet, they noticed the symbol, chopped into the bark and smeared with mud to make it look old.

Once they'd found one, they became easier to spot, and more frequent. It was like following a treasure trail, or hunting for the little painted wooden carrots that used to be hidden in the meadow every Lupen's Day at the start of spring.

Next they had to look out for the stone tree that Brigid had described. Podkin thought this might be just a riddle, until he almost walked into it.

Jutting up from a clutch of bramble bushes, the carved stone was as broad as an ancient oak. It curved at the top, and was spattered all over in crusty patches of overlapping lichen. Stepping back to look at it, Podkin realised it was actually the remains of an arched doorway.

The rabbits stared at it for a while. It was a wonder to them why anyone would build something like this above ground, and how they had even managed to do it. The thing towered over them, sculpted so cleanly. There had been a stone fireplace in the Munbury warren, but everything else had been built out of wood, carved all over with patterns of twining leaves and the daisy that had been their tribal symbol. To make something this big out of stone would have taken such effort; and it was only *part* of a doorway. What had the rest of the building been like?

A voice suddenly echoed out of nowhere, making them all jump. 'Who goes there?' They looked around the darkening woods, trying to spot its owner, but couldn't see anything. Surely it hadn't come from the stone pillar itself?

'Erm ... hello?' Podkin called.

'I said, *who goes there*?' The voice repeated. This time it clearly came from somewhere near the ground. They peered at the roots of the bramble bush and were surprised to see a hole hidden there. A pair of eyes peeked out, staring at them suspiciously.

'Just some children,' said Podkin, remembering what Brigid had told them to say. 'We've come to buy herbs for our master. He gave us a map to follow.' He demonstrated this by waving the piece of bark in the air.

'You won't find many herbs left at this time of year,' said the voice. 'And this is no place for children.'

'Please,' said Paz. 'If you don't let us in, we'll freeze. And if we don't come back with herbs, we'll get beaten.'

'Hmpf,' said the voice. 'Let me see your eyes then.'

At first Podkin thought this was a strange request, but then he realised what the guard was checking for: signs of the red rust of the Gorm. Proof that the evil iron poison hadn't possessed them.

One by one they knelt and stared at the guard-rabbit, pulling their eyelids down so he could see them better. He must have been satisfied, as there was a grunt and the sound of a door being unbolted. All of a sudden, the ground around the hole fell away to reveal a tunnel, lit inside by flickering candles. The owner of the eyes was standing there: a scarred old warrior rabbit with a long braided beard and patched leather armour. He looked like the veteran of several fierce battles, ones in which his enemies ended up with several missing body parts. Podkin wouldn't want to be someone trying to sneak past *him* into Boneroot.

He beckoned them in, all the while keeping one hand on his sword hilt and a frown on his face. 'You can go down, but if you want my advice, buy your herbs and get out quick. There's rabbits down there that'll eat you lot for breakfast. While you're still squeaking too.'

They walked past the guard very quickly, careful to nod him a polite thank you, and emerged into a long tunnel, which sloped steeply downwards. Every warren that Podkin had ever been in had had a grand entrance burrow, paved or tiled, hung with tapestries or plastered and painted. This was just a muddy tunnel, roots poking out the sides, lit by a few smoky candles. What had they just walked into?

Behind them, they heard the door thumping

closed, shutting them inside Boneroot. There was nothing else to do but keep going on down the tunnel and into whatever lay beyond.

*

The first thing Podkin noticed was the smell.

He had grown up in a warren, and no matter how clean and hygienic the rabbits, a large amount of furry bodies in a small enclosed space always gave a certain spice to the air. Especially if there had been turnips for dinner. Or, Goddess have mercy, beetroot curry.

This smell was something completely different. It was more than just an aroma; it was a solid, living wall, and walking down the tunnel was like doing a running leap headfirst into it. It nearly knocked the little rabbits over. Every smell in the world was there, all blended into one musty, meaty, fruity, furry pong.

'Takes yer breath away, don't it?' came the voice of the guard-rabbit behind them, who must have heard their disgusted gasps. They couldn't even reply. Squinting against the stench, they carried on down the tunnel to find just what it was that smelt so bad.

It was rabbits. Hundreds of rabbits.

There were hordes of them, in every shade and colour of fur. Brown rabbits, white rabbits; piebald, skewbald, spotted and brindled. Giant rabbits, towering over the crowds; tiny Elfin dwarves, smaller than children; fluffy-maned Lionheads, spotted Harlequins, velvety Rexs, woolly Angoras. And then many more breeds and tribes that Podkin had never seen or heard of. All these creatures, scared out of their homes by the Gorm. How many of these rabbits felt as lost and alone as he did?

The noise was almost as loud as the smell: a babbling surge of chatter, music and shouting that washed over them as soon as they stepped out of the tunnel and into a huge chamber, in which the swarms of rabbits rattled like beans in a jar.

The stone archway was nothing compared to what Podkin saw now. More pillars of carved and fluted stone stretched down from the chamber ceiling to the floor, holding everything together and allowing this enormous space to exist. It was a colossal cavern: big enough to fit ten longburrows with room to spare.

Up above, the roof was a mass of roots and vines

that twisted down the ancient stone and ran across the chamber floor. The pillars, the roots, the walls – every spare inch of them were draped with lanterns or studded with thick candles that had spilt rivers of melted wax over everything.

In between the stone columns, the rabbits had created the craziest, most bustling market Podkin had ever seen. The place was blurred with stalls and kiosks selling all sorts of goods. There were grand painted booths, tables draped with cloth, and in some places just tatty blankets spread on the floor.

Trader rabbits stood amongst them, behind them, on top of them – haggling and arguing with customers, shouting out their wares and filling the chamber with so much noise it made Podkin's head spin. There was mead for sale; roasted, stewed, fried and boiled vegetables of every description; clay pots, candles, lamps, weapons, clothes, armour, musical instruments, potions, charms, books and scrolls, wooden toys and dolls ... too much to even begin to take in.

Who was in charge here? Who was keeping the order in this crazy mess? He could see no guards or

soldiers anywhere. The whole place was free to do just what it liked, and yet somehow it was working.

The little rabbits stood for several minutes, blinking with wide eyes and trying to take it all in. They suddenly realised that Munbury warren – the place they had thought of as the centre of the world – had actually been a tiny scrap of a home compared to this.

'Wow,' Podkin finally managed to say.

'Yes,' agreed Paz. 'Wow.'

'Soop,' added Pook.

The whole thing reminded Podkin of the Tinker Fair that used to come to Munbury just after Summertide each year. A mismatched collection of wagons and tents, with goods from all over the Five Realms spread out for sale. There were always jugglers too, and acrobats, fire-breathers, stilt-walkers.

'Looks like the Fair, doesn't it?' Paz said, thinking the same thing.

'Do you remember the year Father tried to swallow fire?'

'And he singed his beard right off?'

Podkin started to chuckle, but then he remembered that his father was gone. Instead of laughing, he felt like something was broken. His eyes met Paz's. He knew she felt it too. The world itself was wrong now: incomplete. How could it go on like it always had, with people buying and selling knick-knacks and trinkets, when his father was no longer a part of it?

These rabbits hadn't even known Lopkin of Munbury had existed. The three children stood in silence, letting the sounds and smells of the market wash over them.

'Well,' said Paz, a few moments later. 'Where d'you think we should start looking? For the mercenaries?'

It took Podkin a moment to remember that was why they were here. He forced himself to return to the present and its problems. A mercenary. A guardian. But how were you supposed to find anything in such a nameless jumble of rabbits?

'We could try asking someone?'

'What an amazing idea. You must be some kind of genius.'

'You don't have to be so sarcastic,' said Podkin, scowling. 'Have you got any better ideas?'

'Ideas? What would I have ideas for? I'm not the chieftain, am I? Girls aren't allowed to be chiefs, remember?' Paz tucked Pook under her shoulder and trotted over to speak to the nearest stallholder, a black-furred rabbit selling jars of pickled beetroot, forcing Podkin to scurry after her. 'Excuse me – do you know where we can hire soldiers? Is there a shop or a booth or something?'

'Soldiers? You mean sellswords?' The rabbit looked the children up and down, suspicious. Her eyes seemed to linger on Paz's silver bracelet and Podkin's belt buckle. 'What do you little 'uns need hired thugs for?'

'We're just curious, that's all.' Podkin couldn't think of a convincing lie quickly enough. The rabbit raised an eyebrow and pointed across the hall to a fenced-off area next to one of the pillars.

'Over there. But you won't find much worth hiring. All the fighters I know have been scared off by the Gorm. Fled, they have – less dangerous over the mountains. Can I interest you in a jar of beetroot?'

After politely declining, they edged their way through the crush of bodies until they reached the sellsword stall. They could see a few ragged rabbits lounging around inside the fenced-off area: a broad, muscular buck with long snow-white fur that he wore spiked into porcupine points all over his head, whose left arm and leg were splinted and bandaged. A black-furred giant with torn ears and a missing arm. A brown, spotted Harlequin rabbit with a wooden leg and a crutch.

Podkin's gaze was caught by one grey-furred rabbit with blank white eyes who sat silent and still in a corner. Was that all Boneroot had to offer? Some ragged, worn-out scrappers, one of whom was blind? They would be better off facing the Gorm on their own.

'I don't think much of that lot,' said Podkin.

Paz nodded. 'Me neither. Although I suppose they won't cost much to hire. My bracelet will pay for the lot of them twice over.'

Podkin was about to walk into the enclosure to find out, but he never got the chance. A strong-fingered hand gripped his arm so tightly that it hurt, and he felt the sharp sting of a knife tip pressed against his ribs.

He saw Paz's eyes go wide with fear, and looked up to see an evil-faced rabbit with patchy brown fur and mean orange eyes. He leant over them and whispered with breath that stank of rotten vegetables and stale mead.

'You three little nippers are mine now. And your pretty jewellery too. Come along with me, nice and quiet, or I'll chop this one's other ear off. Snickety snip.'

He grinned, showing yellow broken teeth, and pushed his knife harder into Podkin's chest so that Podkin yelped. There was nothing Paz could do but follow as her brother was dragged off, out of the hall and into the maze of endless side tunnels.

CHAPTER NINE

Shape and Quince

Podkin was dragged deeper and deeper into the Boneroot tunnels, the stinking rabbit's hand tight around his arm, his knife jabbing in his ribs. He could hear Paz following behind, and Pook quietly crying. Every now and then the rabbit looked over his shoulder and made a comment. 'That's it, little girl. You just keep following nicely and I won't have to slice up your brother.'

The further they got from the marketplace, the quieter it was. The noise of the market was still there, but muffled and distant, as if the whole thing had been a dream.

At first there had been some signs of life and light – shop fronts and houses – along the tunnel sides: a pickled-radish vendor; a line of washing hung up to dry; a tavern. But now there was just the odd empty burrow-mouth – dark lonely voids in the tunnel, which was already being slowly choked and filled up with spidery roots. Podkin wondered, in between sharp prickles of the knife in his side, whether the whole world would one day look like that, once rabbitkind had crumbled into dust. The roots, moss and earth would slowly crawl over everything, hiding it away like they had never existed at all.

Every so often they came across a piece of rib, or a jawbone, jutting down from the roof or sticking up out of the floor. People had propped candles on top of some, and they were now decorated with stalactites of dribbled wax. Who did they once belong to? Who buried them? If he wasn't in fear for his life, Podkin might have stopped to ponder it all.

It was damp here: mildewy and rotten. There were piles of mouldering rubbish all over the floor, adding to the stink of decay. Mushrooms grew out of the tunnel sides, glowing pale in the murk, like strange little ghosts or the eyes of lurking monsters. Every now and then, something wriggled on the floor. Fat, pale earthworms or grubs of some kind. Podkin heard Paz step on one. There was a soft *pop*, followed by a muffled squeal. She always had hated creepy crawlies. That's what made it so much fun to hide them in her bed, back in Munbury.

Oh, if only they were back in Munbury.

Podkin thought about trying to draw the dagger and fight the big rabbit off, but it was too tricky to get to. By the time he'd untangled it from its cloth scabbard, the smelly oaf would probably have chopped him into pieces. Then the rabbit would have Starclaw as well. There was absolutely nothing Podkin could do.

Finally they came to a burrow entrance, out at the furthest reaches of the tunnel. There were mounds of rotting scraps piled outside. Half-chewed radishes, shards of broken pottery, sticky pools of mush that might once have been food. The entire floor of the tunnel was heaving and pulsing with maggots.

133

A dim glow seeped out from the doorway. Podkin had a few seconds to wonder what terrors might lie within, and then the smelly rabbit pulled back the tattered blanket that covered the entrance and shoved him through. Paz and Pook were pushed after, crashing into his back and knocking them both to the floor.

'Well, well, what have you caught, Quince?'

Podkin looked up to find himself in a small burrow. A typical living area for most warren rabbits, but one that seemed tiny to him. The walls were bare earth, a patch of old whitewash here and there, but more patches of black mould and bubbling fungus.

There was a large wooden chest by one wall, and two cages made of crudely lashed-together hazel branches against the other. The rest of the floor space was covered with piles of empty and broken clay bottles, gnawed carrot tops and layers of dust and cobwebs. This was a neglected and half-derelict place. It smelt stale and putrid, almost as bad as the tunnel outside.

A small fireplace was hidden amongst the junk, and a few sputtering, smoky logs were burning there, giving the place a hazy orange glow. Sitting beside it, warming his belly, was another rabbit: a huge fat lop, his ears held back by a stained bandana. He had a long braided beard with a silver bell tied at the end, and was watching them with small eyes. By his side was a huge wooden club, studded at one end with rusty spikes and nails.

'I have hit the jackpot, Mister Shape,' said the smelly rabbit, Quince. 'Two posh little bunnies and one little sprogling. Found them peering at the sellswords like they was at a zoo or something.'

'Sellswords, eh? Well, if they wanted to see the best fighter in Boneroot, they only had to come here for a peek.' The fat rabbit stood up, his stomach rolling off his lap to hang about his knees. He wore shoulder pads and leather greaves, but his great scarred belly was bare and as broad as an oak trunk. 'Get them up so I can look at them.'

Podkin felt his good ear being pulled, bringing him to his feet. Paz was yanked up too, squealing in pain. Pook whined and tried to hide in his big sister's tunic.

'Hern's whiskers! Look at that belt buckle!

And that bracelet. They look awful heavy for such little kittens. Perhaps you should lighten their load, Quince.'

The smelly rabbit laughed and roughly pulled off Paz's bracelet. He grabbed Podkin's belt and sawed through the leather with his knife. Podkin wanted to shout about how it had been a Midwinter present from his father, but the look on Mister Shape's face made him keep his mouth shut.

'They got anything else, Quince?'

Podkin felt the weasely rabbit's hand close over Starclaw's scabbard, and the knife was yanked free. He closed his eyes in despair. *The one thing you were told to keep safe, and you couldn't even do that.*

'Just this crummy old butter knife, Mister Shape. Doesn't look fit to trim me toenails with.'

Shape gave it a glance, but he was more interested in the buckle and bracelet that Quince had just tossed him. 'We'll consider that your first night's rent paid,' said Shape. 'You can keep that toy knife for now. You couldn't do any harm with it anyway. And it might come in handy for cutting purses. After all, you'll be earning your room and board in future.' Both the nasty rabbits laughed hard at this joke, although Podkin had no idea what it meant. 'Show them their room, Quince.'

The smelly rabbit went over to the wooden cages. He pulled open the door to one, and the three little rabbits were kicked inside.

'Just in case you are thinking of sneaking out in the night,' said Mister Shape, 'you should know one of us is always awake, watching you very closely.'

Quince cackled and waved his knife in the candlelight so it sparkled, leaving the rabbits in no doubt as to what would happen to them if they tried to escape. As the evil rabbits laughed some more, Podkin and Paz looked at each other, wide-eyed and terrified.

*

The rest of that night felt endless, uncomfortable and frightening. Podkin and Paz sat in their little cage, staring out at the burrow where Quince and Shape sat, while Pook snuggled between them, whining for food. Once or twice they tried to whisper to each other, but the two villains always heard them. Quince had a long stick he used to poke and prod them through the bars, trying his best to crack them on the heads or shins where it really hurt. In the end they gave up trying to speak, and just sat in miserable silence.

Podkin noticed the huddled shape of two other rabbits in the second cage. Small ones. Children like him, probably. They had obviously learnt not to make any sound. Once he thought that he glimpsed an eye peeking at him before blinking shut again. He wondered how long they had been there, trapped without anyone to rescue them. The thought made him shudder.

After Goddess knows how long, Pook whimpered himself to sleep, Paz too seemed to have drifted off, and snores started to come from the two big rabbits guarding them on the other side of the bars. *This is my chance*, Podkin thought. *But what can I do?*

Podkin's scared little mind whirred, trying to think of a plan, but came up with nothing. *What would Father have done?* He tried to listen for the reassuring voice inside his head, but there was only silence. *Would he have sat here and waited for what misery morning would bring?* Never. By now, he would probably have sliced through the bars and run charging at the villains, ready to chop them into rabbit hotpot.

Well *that* wasn't going to happen. He had missed every single one of his weapons lessons. He barely knew the handle of a sword from the pointy end. But maybe he could cut a small hole in the bars for them to sneak out? It sounded like a much better plan, with a lot less slicing.

He thought he might be able to slide Starclaw out from under his cloak and chop through the cage bars, and was just inching his hand across to do it when a voice from the shadows outside made him freeze.

'I'm still awake, you little rat-weasel,' came Shape's deep, rumbling tones. 'And I'll be awake for the next two hours, until it's Quince's turn to watch you. You'll not get away that easy.'

The fat rabbit chuckled to himself, and settled back to sipping mead, or whatever he was doing. Sure enough, ages later, he nudged Quince awake, and lay down to sleep on a scrap of blanket.

Quince is smaller, Podkin thought. *Maybe I could get out and lop off his head before he could wake up Shape?* But he knew he wouldn't do it. Toppling a tree on someone is one thing; chopping a rabbit's head off would be unbearable.

Waiting 'til morning it is then. Podkin couldn't help but feel he'd failed some kind of test. But then he was well used to failing tests. In fact, he was probably an expert at it.

Sorry, Father. I'm just not a hero like you. He rubbed the bare spot where his belt buckle had been and dreamt memories of the Bramblemas day he had unwrapped it, with his proud father smiling on.

*

Come morning, a bleary-eyed, exhausted Podkin sat in a corner of the cage. Paz and Pook had both had a pretty good night's sleep, all things considered. But Podkin had barely managed to catch a wink. Noises from outside the cage had stirred them, and the three rabbits gave each other nervous glances, wondering what horrible thing was going to happen next.

Both Shape and Quince were up now. They opened the cage door and dragged Podkin out by his collar. The little rabbit stood in the dingy burrow, swaying on his feet, while they pulled another rabbit out of the second cage. It was a tiny brown rabbit with a fuzzy cotton ball of a face and pointy little ears. Another, just like it, peered sadly through the cage bars.

'Listen up, new boy,' said Mister Shape, bending down over his fat belly to peer in Podkin's face. 'You're going to go back to the market to spend the rest of this lovely day begging, scrounging and stealing everything you can get your little paws on.'

'Food, we want,' said Quince. 'And drink. And money. And anything we can sell to make money.'

'Basically,' Shape continued, 'we want you to fill your pockets with as much stuff as you can, and then bring it back here to us.'

'And if I don't?' Podkin asked. He didn't like the sound of stealing, much less coming back to this stinking ferret-hole of a burrow.

'Why, if you don't, then we might get hungry and decide to eat your big sister,' said Quince.

'A nice little snack she'd make, eh, Quincey?' said Shape, his broad belly rippling with laughter. Podkin gulped. Shape, suddenly serious again, grabbed him by the collar and pulled him close.

'She's our insurance.' He growled in Podkin's face. 'Keeping her safe is what makes you come back here every day.'

'Every day?'

'Oh yes.' Shape gave an evil grin. 'You work for us now. And you're going to be working for us for a *very* long time.'

In the cage, Pook started crying. And crying. And crying. It got louder and louder, until it became a piercing wail. Paz tried to quieten him, afraid of Quince's jabbing stick, but he wouldn't shush, not even when Paz mentioned soup. She looked out at Podkin, scared.

'Shut that brat up!' Shape yelled. 'Or by Hern's hairy kneecaps, I'll do it for you!' Quince made to grab for his stick, so Podkin quickly spoke.

'He won't be quiet, not as long as he's in that cage,' he said. 'I'll have to take him with me. You won't hear him then, and you've still got my sister to make sure I come back.'

He wasn't sure what he was going to do with Pook, exactly; he just knew he had to get him away from Quince and Shape. Perhaps the pair of them could escape somehow? Come back with help for Paz? But there was nobody who would help them, now that they had no money to bargain with.

'Take him then,' Shape shouted. 'Just stop that flaming screeching!'

Quince opened the cage door and pulled Pook out of Paz's arms, then swung him at Podkin. Podkin just about managed to catch his little brother and at least the shock had stopped him crying for a moment.

'Right. Enough of this chin-wagging,' said Shape. 'Get out there and get us some loot.'

With several nudges from his bony foot, Quince shoved Podkin and the other rabbit out of the burrow and into the tunnel, then pulled the blanket shut. Podkin managed to catch Paz's eyes for a moment as he left. She looked lonely, sad, frightened – but she had enough time to motion to him. A small, flicking movement with her fingers. *Run*, she meant. *Go. Leave.*

She was telling him to take Pook and not come back.

CHAPTER TEN

Fox Paw

Outside in the gloomy tunnel, Podkin stood and stared at the other little rabbit. She stared back for a moment, then shrugged her shoulders and hurried off down the tunnel, towards the market.

'Hey, wait up!' Podkin scampered after as best he could, struggling not to drop Pook in the process. He caught up with the rabbit by a flickering candle, which was balanced on the crumbling tip of some creature's leg bone, jutting out of the tunnel wall. The light threw wavering patterns over the dangling roots and piles of rubbish on the floor, making it seem like they were at the bottom of a particularly filthy lake.

The small rabbit gave him another impatient look, as if Podkin was keeping her from something important. 'Yes?'

Podkin stood, huffing and puffing, thinking of something to say. 'Um . . . hello. My name's Podkin. And this is Pook. I just . . . I was just wondering . . .'

'Look,' said the rabbit. 'I don't mean to be rude, but we really should get to the market as quickly as we can. If we don't come back at dusk with plenty of food and some coins . . . well, let's just say it won't be very pleasant.'

'Do you do this every day?' Podkin asked. 'Stealing and begging from the market? Haven't you tried to escape?'

'Escape?' The little rabbit looked at Podkin as if he was crazy. 'They've got my brother. How could I escape without him?'

'But your parents,' said Pod. 'Can't you find them? Can't you tell the guards or the chieftain or someone?'

'My parents are fifty years old and living in a warren on the other side of the Eiskalt mountains.' When Podkin looked at her as if she was talking Thriantan, she sighed and shook her head. 'I'm not a *child*, Popkin – or whatever your name is. My brother and I are dwarf rabbits. I might be as small as you, but I'm actually fully grown. Those stupid ferret-brained lumps back there think we're children too. That's why they grabbed us.'

'Have you been there long?'

The dwarf rabbit shrugged. 'Six months, I think. Although it seems like longer. They had another rabbit caged up when we got there, but he got sick and died. They buried him further up the tunnel.'

Podkin gulped. He really didn't want to end up shovelled into a shallow grave in this dingy, miserable place.

'So, you see, it's best to try and keep them happy. That way they don't hit you. Try and find as much food as you can, but don't get caught stealing anything. There aren't any guards in this place, and definitely no chieftain, but the stallholders do horrible things to thieves.'

The dwarf rabbit patted Podkin on the shoulder, and then turned and headed up the tunnel. Podkin watched her go, calling out before she disappeared from sight: 'It's *Podkin*, not Popkin!'

'Sorry!' The rabbit called back. 'I'm Mishka. But you can call me Mish. My brother is Mashka.' And then she was gone.

Mish and Mash, Podkin thought. Well, at least they weren't in this mess completely on their own.

'Mish!' said Pook.

*

Some time later, Podkin and Pook stepped out of the side tunnel and into the market hall once more. Again, he was hit by the wall of stink and noise, although this time his nose was a little more used to it. He could actually pick out some smells: spices, frying vegetables, roasted coffee, tanned leather, burning incense; each one fought with the other, trying not to be overpowered, and making his head spin.

He stared out at the heaving mass of rabbits, all bustling about their business. From somewhere out there, he had to find enough food and coins to keep Shape and Quince happy, and avoid getting caught and strung up by the ears (or ear) in the process. He felt sick with fear. To top it all, his arms were already weak and burning from carrying and dragging Pook down the tunnel, and he had never stolen anything in his life. His mother always used to say that the Goddess thought very poorly of thieves and robbers. Would she understand if a little rabbit was doing it to save his sister's life?

His eyes drifted across the seething marketplace to the entrance tunnel, which was little more than a dark hole across the crowded cavern. Did Paz really want them to leave without her? Could he even do such a thing? She was his big sister. Annoying, yes. Bossy, definitely. But she was near enough the only family he had left. And he did love her very much (even though he would never admit it).

Besides, she was the one with all the ideas – the quick thinker, always coming up with a plan in an instant. He was just the lazy, spoilt chieftain's son, daydreaming and snoozing around until he became head of the tribe and could daydream and snooze even more. He wouldn't last ten minutes looking after Pook by himself.

Paz would never leave me behind, he thought. *So I'm not going to leave her.* He took a deep breath and began to look around for something to steal.

So, where should he start? Cutting some rabbit's

purse? That was obviously what Shape expected him to do, leaving him Starclaw. He had no idea how to go about it, though. And what if you got caught? *The stallholders do horrible things to thieves*, Mish had said. He wondered what that could be. Throwing them in a dungeon? Sticking red-hot pokers into their squidgy bits? Chopping off their hands? He'd already lost an ear so he really should start being more careful about holding on to his body parts.

How about grabbing something from a stall? There were hot pies over there, and next to it a rabbit selling clay jugs of mead. Was he fast enough to snatch something and run for it? Not with having to carry Pook as well. Maybe he should have left him crying in the cage. Perhaps if Shape had got sick enough of the noise, he might have let them all go.

'Soop!' Pook said. 'Soop! Soop!'

'You're not having any soup,' Podkin told him, but there was a soup-seller nearby, and the delicious smell was everywhere.

'Soop!' Pook screamed. Podkin started to pull his little brother away from the tempting odours, round behind a stone pillar where the air was more dank and musty. But it didn't have any effect on Pook's howling, which was getting louder, if anything. What did his mother use to do when this happened? Smack his bottom? Shove a rotten turnip in his mouth?

No, she used to distract him with something. Take his mind off his stomach for a moment until he forgot what he was screaming about.

'Look, Pook. Over there! A really fat rabbit selling carrots . . .'

'Ca-ot! Ca-ot!'

'No, no . . . bad example. Look over there! A big lop rabbit! Look at his long ears, and on his stall he's got . . . oh.'

'Hu-ny! Hu-ny!'

Podkin felt like crying. He sank to the floor, amongst all the muck and rubbish from the market, and let Pook's shouts merge with the noise of the stalls into one big thunderous racket. There was no way he could find enough loot to keep Quince happy. There was no way he could escape Boneroot along with his brother and sister, and even if he did, the Gorm were looking for him everywhere. What was the point? He might as well just lay here in the dirt until he starved to death and . . .

Something hard was under his leg. Something round and hard. Something round and hard and coin-shaped.

Holding his breath, he dug his paw into the grime and muck beneath him and fished it out. It looked like a lump of sticky old mud, but when he rubbed it against his cloak, the unmistakeable glint of metal shone through.

'Oooh!' Pook said. 'Shiny!'

Quickly, Podkin polished off the rest of the dirt. It was a large coin, marked with a rabbit's head and made of an orangey-brown metal. Copper, he thought, or bronze. Having never worried about money before, he wasn't sure what it was worth. Not as much as gold or silver, definitely, but might it be enough to satisfy Quince and Shape?

'This is good, Pook,' he said. 'But we need more, I think. Can you help me find some more?'

'Shiny!' Pook squealed, and started rummaging around in the dirt and rotten food of the market floor. Surely there had to be more coins hidden in all this litter, and scavenging for it was much safer than stealing. Podkin got on his hands and knees and joined him.

*

An hour later, they had covered half of the market, scrabbling about in the dirt between the stalls. Podkin had been kicked in the ribs by two stallholders and chased off by several more. And they had nothing to show for it except an old apple core, which Pook was now sucking on. That and the original copper coin. So much for his get-rich-quick idea.

'This is not good, Pook,' he said.

The little rabbit wasn't listening. Something had caught his attention on the other side of the market. 'Bone! Bone!'

Pook had dropped his soggy apple core and was pointing excitedly at a dingy corner. Three or four scruffy-looking rabbits were crouched in a circle, taking turns to roll dice. Some kind of game, Podkin supposed.

'Bone!' Pook started crawling over. The dice must have reminded him of the casting bones he'd played with at Brigid's place. He was drawn to them in the same way.

Podkin didn't think the scruffy rabbits would take

kindly to a strange baby ruining their game. He jumped up and ran after Pook, grabbing him just before he managed to snatch up the dice in his chubby little paw.

'Oi, nibbler! Keep your brat out of our game!' A black and white rabbit with torn ears and brown teeth tried to slap at Pook as Podkin pulled him back.

'Yeah,' said another scrawny brown buck. 'Unless he wants to join in!'

Three of the rabbits roared with laughter, while the fourth looked miserable. He threw a handful of copper coins on to the floor and the others snatched them up. Podkin stared. A whole *handful* of coins.

'Are you playing for money?' he asked. He remembered seeing guards back at the warren doing something like this. His mother never allowed him to watch too closely.

'Fox Paw. Winner takes all,' said the brown rabbit. 'Care to chance your luck?'

Fox Paw. The name rang a bell. Wasn't it from that story Brigid had told them? The dice game the Goddess herself had played when she beat Gormaduke, or whatever he had been called. Surely that must be a sign?

A foolish rabbit and his radishes are easily

parted. That was what Auntie Olwyn always used to say. Or was it his mother? Someone much more sensible than him, anyway. It meant that gambling was for ferret-brains. They'd only managed to find one single coin all morning, and here he was thinking of throwing it away.

But . . . Pook had been so good at rolling the bones on Brigid's hearth. *A natural gift,* she'd said. And the little tinker was itching to do it again. What if it *was* a sign from the Goddess? He looked at the piles of coins lined up in front of the rabbits. *It is a stupid thing to do*, he thought, *but there's nobody around to tell me otherwise.* Just for once, he could be as stupid as he liked, and what if it worked?

'We're in,' he said, holding out his copper coin. 'But my brother gets to roll for me.'

The scruffy rabbits hooted and roared at this, so much that others wandered over to see what was going on. Soon there was a little crowd around the game, with Pook in the middle trying to grab at the dice.

'Let's play then,' said the brown rabbit. 'D'you know the rules?' When Podkin shook his head, he laughed even harder. 'There's three dice, see? Bone ones, with six sides apiece. They're marked with a one, a two, a three, four, five and a fox's paw. Each time you roll, you add the numbers up. You can roll as many times as you like, but if you get one single fox paw, you're out. The one with the highest score at the end wins the money. Understand?'

Podkin nodded. Basically, you didn't want to roll a fox paw. Simple.

The black and white rabbit sneered at him. 'Seeing as it's your first game, you can start.'

'Roll, Pook,' Podkin said. The crowd behind him gave a little cheer. Pook grabbed the dice with glee and threw them down.

A whoop went up from the crowd, and Podkin realised he had been scrunching his eyes shut. He looked down to see two threes and a one.

'Beginner's luck,' said the brown rabbit. 'Roll again?'

Perhaps they should stop and keep the score, Podkin thought. He had no idea of what a good total was. If they rolled again, they risked losing everything. But that was what games of chance were all about, weren't they?

'Go on, Pook. Roll again.'

The little rabbit snatched the dice up and flung them. For one horrible moment, Podkin was sure there would be fox paws showing, but the crowd cheered again. A pair of twos and a three.

'Eleven,' said the brown rabbit. He was starting to look less amused. 'Roll again, why don't you? It's easy to get higher than that.'

'Stop there!' someone from the crowd called out. Other voices joined in: 'They'll never beat that!' 'Eleven's amazing!' 'The Goddess herself only rolled 9!' Podkin began to pull Pook back, but he had grabbed the dice again. He threw them in the air, chortling with joy.

'Pook!' Podkin yelled. He watched the dice spinning in slow motion, tumbling to the muddy floor and bouncing up and down again. Surely, this time, there would be a fox's paw showing. Instead, there were three fives.

'Cheat!' The black and white rabbit yelled. 'You must be cheating!'

The crowd behind Podkin booed and shouted at the black and white rabbit, and he quickly backed down. He folded his arms and shot evil looks at Podkin across the circle.

'Have another go, little one,' the brown rabbit cooed at Pook, trying to make him lose his score. 'One more roll. It's such fun, isn't it?'

Podkin tightened his grip on Pook, but the little rabbit didn't even move to touch the dice. Instead, he wrapped his arms about his podgy legs and stared at the scruffy rabbits, as if daring them to go next.

The child's a born gambler, Podkin thought, amazed.

Seeing Pook's turn was over, the other rabbits tried their luck. The brown rabbit rolled a fox paw first time, as did the black and white. The third scruffy rabbit managed a second roll before he threw three fox paws together. There were cheers and whoops from all the onlookers. 'Pay up!' they called. 'Pay them their due!'

With sulky faces, the scruffy rabbits each handed over a copper coin. The money chinked heavily in Podkin's outstretched paws. By some miracle, he had turned one coin into five, when by rights he should be walking away with nothing.

'Shiny!' Pook said.

Interlude

The bard stops talking and pauses for a moment to tug his beard. He gives his audience a thoughtful look. 'I suppose I should say a few words to you about gambling, and how it's a very stupid thing to do.'

'Podkin the Great did it,' says the inquisitive rabbit. 'And he was a hero.'

'And the Goddess herself,' added the sensible rabbit. 'And *she* is a goddess. Obviously.'

'My Uncle Colm does it all the time,' says another rabbit. 'He won a whole keg of mead once.'

'My daddy won a spear and a shield and a cloak and some trousers. In fact, everything the other rabbit was wearing.'

'Yes, yes, yes.' The bard waves his hands to stop the chattering. 'I'm sure lots of people have won lots of things, including the Goddess herself. But for everything they won, I bet ... I mean, I'm *sure* ... they lost even more. Pook won because he had a touch of magic about him when it came to casting bones. Not many other rabbits have that blessing. Whatever tales of glory you've heard, gambling is for idiots.'

A cheer comes from the corner of the room where the guards are playing dice. The doorman has come off duty and seems to be winning.

The bard shrugs. 'I rest my case.'

'We get the picture,' says the sensible rabbit. 'Don't gamble. Now what did Podkin do with the money?'

The bard smiles and continues.

Chapter Eleven

Sellswords

If you recall me saying, Podkin didn't know much about money and what it was worth. He was a chieftain's son, and everything he'd ever wanted had been his without having to pay for it. A spoilt brat, some might say. But now that he'd had a sour taste of real life, those five copper coins clutched in his paw seemed like all the treasure in the world.

He tucked them inside his cloak and swiftly pulled Pook away from the dingy corner, back into the market throng. The last thing he wanted was those scruffy rabbits trying to steal their money back, so he spent a while dodging to and fro, hiding behind stalls, roots and crumbling pillars. Once they were good and lost he stopped to think.

What should he do with his winnings? Give it all to Quince and Shape? The thought made him sick. Maybe he could give them a few coins and keep the rest hidden? But then they might search him ...

He could buy Pook and himself something to eat, then take them the rest? Then he thought of poor Paz, shut up in that cage on her own, cold and scared and lonely. Spending money on themselves would just be selfish.

Looking around for inspiration, he saw that they were standing near the sellsword enclosure. The group of mercenaries were identical to the ones on show the last time they were here, and the agent was still sprawled by the gate, calling out his business with as much enthusiasm as a bored snail.

'Hired swords. Hired swords,' he mumbled. 'The fiercest fighters in the whole of the Five Realms. The greatest warriors in ... whatever. Some of them fought somebody else once upon a time, and apparently they were quite good. Better than average, at least ...'

Business must be slow with that kind of patter, Podkin thought. They'd be glad of any coin. With his five coppers, he might be able to hire the lot. Then he could take them back to Mister Shape's burrow and watch them make matching fur coats out of him and Quince.

Before he really knew what he was doing, he had marched up to the agent and prodded him in the belly.

'Excuse me,' Podkin said, in his best regal voice. 'Would you be the rabbit to see about hiring some mercenaries?'

The agent looked him up and down for a moment, and then roared with laughter. He didn't stop until tears were running down his face.

'That's very funny, kid, but go and play your games somewhere else. I'm trying to do business here.'

'It doesn't look like it,' said Podkin, with a sniff. 'I want to hire your men. All of them.' He pulled the coins from his cloak and held them out to the agent.

'Five coins? Five *whole* copper coins?'

'That's right,' said Podkin. 'Consider this your lucky day.'

'Ha!' The agent was about to laugh again, then

began to look irritated instead. 'Five poxy coppers? Do you know what that's worth? It'd get you half a mouldy carrot and a jug of ditchwater if you were lucky. It's not enough for a single one of my men! Goddess above, I don't know whether to laugh at you or clip your ears. Sorry . . . ear.'

'Not a single one?' Podkin's lovely visions of rescuing Paz and watching Shape and Quince get flattened vanished in a puff of smoke.

'Well, I say that . . .' the agent scratched his head. 'It'd get you *him*.' He pointed to the corner where the grey-furred, blank-eyed rabbit sat on his tattered blanket. 'For an afternoon.'

Podkin stared. A blind soldier rabbit for an afternoon. It was hardly the help and protection that Brigid promised they'd find. Could it even be enough to free Paz and give them the chance to escape Boneroot? Probably not, but what other choice did he have?

'I'll take him,' he said, handing over the money.

*

'Crom,' the grey rabbit said. 'My name is Crom.'

'And have you been a soldier long?' They were

standing just outside the sellsword enclosure, with Podkin craning his neck to look up at his new employee. Pook was trying to climb one of his legs. The grey rabbit, Crom, just stared straight ahead with those blank white eyes.

'Yes. Very long.'

His fur was criss-crossed with old scars, and his armour was dented and scratched. He looked like he'd seen a good deal of fighting, for sure, although Podkin wasn't sure how you could fight when you couldn't even see. 'But what about . . . your eyes?'

'I fought for a long time before this happened,' said Crom. 'And I can fight now. Just . . . differently.' Podkin nodded, still not convinced. The grey rabbit didn't seem bothered. He cleared his throat. 'May I ask you a question?'

'Um, yes?' Podkin said.

'Why is it you want to hire a sellsword, anyway? I can tell you're only a child. You shouldn't even be in a lowdown place like this.'

'Some rabbits have my sister,' Podkin said. 'They've got her shut in a cage, so that I'd come out here and steal stuff for them. I need you to set her free, so that we can get out of this place.'

'Shape and Quince?' Crom said.

'Yes! Do you know them?'

'I've heard of them,' said the grey rabbit. He shrugged. 'I hear a lot of things.'

'Do you think you can beat them?' Podkin asked. 'I mean – Mister Shape is pretty big.'

'I can take care of myself,' said Crom, patting the sword at his side. It looked well-used and sharp. Bigger and scarier than Starclaw, although it didn't look as if it was magic.

'We'd better go then,' said Podkin, peeling Pook off Crom's leg. 'Before my time runs out.'

*

Somehow, they found the tunnel that Pod had emerged from earlier, and started walking back into the damp, musty darkness. Podkin led the way, glancing back now and then to see Crom walking with his arms outstretched, fingers tracing lightly along the earthen walls.

Halfway down, Podkin started struggling with Pook, and the little rabbit began to whimper with hunger.

'Give him here,' said Crom, and he hoisted him on to his broad back. Pook clung there, nuzzled against the scarred fur and gradually nodded off to sleep. Podkin thought it was worth the five coppers not to have to carry the little rabbit any more.

They had only gone a bit further when Crom suddenly stopped and looked behind them, his hand on his sword hilt.

'What is it?' Podkin asked.

'Someone's coming up the tunnel,' Crom whispered.

Podkin squinted back down towards the market. He could just about make out the silhouette of something hopping and scuttling back there. It grew closer as he watched, until he could see it was the dwarf rabbit – his fellow captive – scurrying after them as fast as he could run.

'Popkin,' she managed to gasp when she reached them. 'What ... what's going on? Who are you taking back to the burrow?'

'*Pod*kin,' corrected Pod. 'And this is Crom. He's a soldier I've hired to give Shape and Quince a good kicking.'

'To fight *Shape*?' said Mish. 'But your sellsword is ... I mean he can't—'

'It doesn't matter that he can't see,' Podkin interrupted. 'He's still going to beat them. Aren't you, Crom?' There was a grunt from the darkness behind and above him. Podkin thought it sounded confident, although it didn't really matter. He'd thought of a way to give Crom an edge – quite literally.

'Are you sure about this?' Mish said. 'If it goes wrong, there's no telling what Shape and Quince will do. My brother ...'

'It won't go wrong,' said Podkin. 'I promise. And we'll make sure both our siblings are freed.'

'If you can do that,' said Mish, 'I'll be in your debt forever.'

*

For the rest of the walk to the burrow, Podkin silently prayed to the Goddess that his plan would work. For the second time today he was about to gamble everything on a hunch. Either the Goddess herself was guiding him, or the stress of the past few days had driven him round the twist. He hoped it was the first option.

The tunnel grew darker and damper. Just as the stink of mildew and mushrooms became almost overpowering, they arrived at the blanket-covered entrance.

The three of them (four, if you included Pook) stood silently outside for a few moments, listening. Someone was snoring, and there was the crackle of a small fire. Every now and then there was a rustle of movement, and once or twice Podkin thought he heard a soft, sad sigh that might belong to Paz.

Just as Crom was reaching out to push through the blanket, Podkin stopped him – his little hand tiny against the big warrior's arm.

'Wait,' he whispered, as quietly as he could. 'I want you to use this.'

Struggling with his cloak, Podkin managed to uncover the hilt of Starclaw and pull it out of its scabbard. He felt the familiar warm tingle of the metal, and was suddenly reluctant to let a strange person touch it. It was *his*. His only. What if the big rabbit never gave it back?

It's all right, Podkin. You can trust him. It was

almost as if his father was there, whispering in his ear, telling him what to do. Podkin swallowed hard and gave up the blade, knowing it was for the best. He pressed it into Crom's calloused hand.

The sellsword weighed it, twisted it and ran his fingers over the hilt. In his grip it looked too small and puny to do any damage. He knelt to whisper back to Podkin. 'I have my own sword, boy. This is just a little dagger.'

'Yes,' Podkin replied. 'But I want you to use that one. It's very special. And besides, I'm still your boss, aren't I? At least until the end of the afternoon.'

Crom shrugged. He scooped Pook off his back and handed him to Podkin, then swept aside the blanket and stepped through.

*

There was a grunt of surprise from the burrow beyond. Podkin and Mish dashed through in time to see Quince standing in the centre of the room, his mouth hanging open. The scrawny rabbit was clutching his prodding-stick; he looked like he was just about to give Paz a jab or two through the bars of her cage.

171

'Hern's bristly britches,' he cursed. 'What's going—'

He never got to finish the sentence, as Crom strode right up and cracked him between the ears with Starclaw's hilt. There was a hollow clonking sound, and Quince folded up into a senseless heap on the floor.

'Podkin!' Paz jumped up and grabbed the bars of her cage. Pod had time to flash her a grin, and then there was a roaring from the far side of the burrow. Shape had been sleeping there, clutching a half-drunk bottle of mead. Now he was up, staring at Crom and roaring at the top of his voice.

'You! You're that blind rabbit nobody wants to hire! What in Hern's name are you doing here? And why'd you knock out my partner?'

'I'm acting on behalf of my client,' said Crom. 'And if you know what's good for you, you'll let all these little rabbits go.'

'Your *client*?' Shape gave Podkin an astonished look. For a moment, Pod thought he might give in, but instead he reached for his giant club and flexed his shoulders.

'I'm going to kill you, blind rabbit. Then I'm

going to take your client, turn him inside out and wear him as a hat.'

Podkin gulped. In his head, on the way here, Crom had seemed so huge and strong. Now, standing a few paces away from the hulking Mister Shape, he didn't look half as impressive.

'What have you done, Pod?' Paz hissed from her cage.

He cringed. 'I think I've just turned myself into some very unpleasant headgear.'

Shape charged then, roaring as he came. His spiked club, Beatrice, whistled through the air towards Crom's head. Crom just stood there, motionless. Podkin had a vision of the club knocking off his block, as if he were a particularly realistic snow rabbit, but at the last minute he stepped to one side and raised Starclaw to parry the blow. Of course, as the club was made of wood, the magic dagger sliced through it like it was a giant cucumber.

The severed part of the club flew off and embedded itself in the top of Paz's cage. Suddenly off balance, Shape stumbled – a look of pure surprise on his face. He managed to keep himself upright, staring at the severed piece of club in his hands. His pause gave Crom the chance to twist himself around in a spinning movement, bringing one of his powerful legs up at the same time to kick Shape in the chest. The huge rabbit went flying backwards, crashing into the earthen wall of the burrow, smashing a hole right through and bringing half the ceiling cascading down to bury him.

In less than a few seconds, the fight was over.

There was a stunned silence, and then Podkin, Mish, Paz – and even the caged Mash – started cheering and whooping. Podkin took Starclaw back from Crom and used it to cut open both the cages. Paz rushed out and hugged him hard, tears in her eyes, and then Mash hugged him as well. There was so much hugging going on, Podkin almost turned to hug Crom, but the grey rabbit was standing so silently and solemnly that he thought better of it.

'I can't believe it! I can't believe it!' Mash shouted. 'We're free! We're free!'

'As I promised, I am forever in your debt,'

said Mish to Podkin, bowing so low, her little ears brushed the floor. Mash did the same, and Pod noticed they were almost identical, the only difference being the delicate black tips on the end of Mish's ears.

'It wasn't me,' said Podkin. 'I mean, *I* didn't do anything. It was all Crom.'

Mish and Mash bowed at the warrior rabbit as well, but he appeared not to notice. Instead, he knelt to speak to Podkin.

'That dagger,' he said. 'It wouldn't happen to be magic, would it?'

'Magic?' Podkin stammered for a moment, realising he might have made a mistake in revealing the sacred weapon to someone five times the size of him who was able to knock out two violent criminals in the time it took to peel a carrot. 'Whatever do you mean?'

'Your dagger cut through that club like it was made of air. I've only seen one weapon that could do that, and it was one of the sacred Twelve.' Crom reached out a hand and gripped Podkin by the shoulder. Not a firm grip yet, but one which could squish him like a grape should it be required. 'Tell me how you came by it, boy. Tell me the *truth*.'

Podkin looked into those blank eyes, wondering what kind of story he could come up with that would explain Starclaw. In the end, he realised there was no story. He had had enough of gambling and bluffing for one day, anyway. He would tell the truth, and if he ended up getting kicked through a wall too, so be it.

'It's my father's,' he said, in a quiet voice. 'He is ... *was* ... a chieftain. Of Munbury warren, to the west of here. And you're right. It *is* magic. It can cut through anything in the world. Except iron.'

'Your father then. Is he ...?'

'Dead.' Podkin felt hot tears run from his eyes into his fur. 'The Gorm killed him, at least, we think so. Now it's my dagger, and they're trying to kill me too.'

The room was silent for a moment. Podkin stared at Crom, wondering what was going on in his head. Was he planning to kill them himself and take Starclaw? Or turn them over to the Gorm and collect a fat reward? He was a mercenary, after all.

Finally, Crom spoke. His voice was soft, almost gentle. Not gruff and harsh like it had been before.

'I knew your father, Podkin. I knew him well. We fought together many times, right up until he became chieftain of his warren. He was a good rabbit and a good friend.'

'He . . . he was?'

'Yes. And he would not have wanted to see his children lost in a place like this, running for their lives.'

Still kneeling, Crom drew his own sword. Podkin wondered what the blind warrior was going to do with it. There was nothing left to fight, surely? But Crom simply turned it over, holding the hilt out to Podkin and bowing his head.

'I offer you my service, Podkin, son of Lopkin. My life and my sword are yours to command.'

Not sure what to do, Podkin touched the sword lightly and muttered a thank you. Crom nodded, stood and sheathed his weapon. He still looked fierce, but a little friendlier somehow.

Podkin gave him a smile, even though he knew he couldn't see it. 'Does this mean I get a refund?'

Crom surprised them all by throwing back his head and laughing. 'It means I don't have to sell my skills any more, thank the Goddess.'

'This is all very nice,' said Mash, still holding his sister in a tight hug. 'But can we leave now? We want to get as far away from this stinking place as we can and never come back.'

'That makes six of us,' said Paz. 'I don't know what Brigid was doing, sending us here. I thought she was so wise and clever ...'

Podkin looked up at the serious, deadly face of Crom. 'Maybe she still is, sis,' he said. *Maybe there's been a reason behind everything that's happened today.*

From the ruined corner of the room, Shape gave a groan and his fat belly jiggled, sending more chunks of earth tumbling down on to his head. The rabbits looked at each other and nodded. Time to be somewhere else.

They were just heading out of the door, when the booming sound of a horn blast echoed down the tunnel. It was followed by another, then another.

'What's that?' Podkin asked.

'The Boneroot alarm,' Crom replied. 'Someone has forced their way past the entrance.'

'Who could it be?' Podkin thought he knew the answer even as the words left his mouth. By the terrified look on everyone's faces, they all did too.

'We have to get out of here,' said Paz. 'Right now.'

CHAPTER TWELVE

The Burning

Crom headed straight for the doorway, throwing the curtain aside. From the tunnel came the alarm again. Could Podkin hear the sound of clanking armour as well, or was that his imagination? He felt his heart begin to pound against the flimsy bones of his chest.

'Wait!' Mish shouted. 'Our weapons!'

The two dwarf rabbits ran to a battered wooden box that leant against the crumbling wall of Shape and Quince's hovel. They threw open the lid and began to rummage inside, flinging copper coins, cut purses and empty mead jugs everywhere.

Finally, they pulled out an odd selection of items and began putting them on. Both had two bandoliers made of soft leather and covered in tiny buttoned pouches. Mash also had a long piece of wooden pipe, and Mish grabbed a wooden catapult. She tested the rubber on it and grinned.

'There's more weapons,' she said. 'You should arm yourselves.'

Podkin waved Starclaw in answer, but Paz ran to the box and dragged out a bronze short sword. She swished it through the air a couple of times.

'What've you got that for?' Podkin asked. 'You don't even know how to use it!'

'I do.'

'How? Mother would never let you loose with a deadly weapon! She wanted you to learn weaving and embroidery.'

'I got Melfry the weaponmaster to teach me,' said Paz. 'Whenever he couldn't find *you*, because you were off snoozing somewhere.'

Toasted turnips! Podkin thought. *That would have amounted to quite a few lessons. She's probably pretty good.* He nodded at his sister with a grudging admiration as she turned to follow Crom out of the burrow. Now was not the time for a squabble.

Before leaving, he had a quick rummage in the box and pulled out Paz's silver bracelet and his belt buckle. Goddess-be-damned if he was going to leave them behind for Shape and Quince. He tucked them into his cloak pocket and hurried after the others.

The small group stepped out of the doorway, weapons at the ready. Crom scooped Pook on to his back and ran a paw along the mildewy earthen wall. 'Does this tunnel lead anywhere? An exit? Somewhere to hide?' He sounded like a soldier now – a captain about to lead his troops into battle.

Mish and Mash both shook their heads. 'It's a dead end down that way,' said Mash. 'Just a load of rubbish and slops.'

'Then we have to go back into the main chamber. Everyone stay behind me and don't get separated,' Crom ordered. It was the last thing they wanted to hear, but they fell in line all the same.

The tunnel seemed longer and scarier than ever.

Noises floated towards them that were nothing to do with the market. Snatches of shouting, shrieks of fear. Podkin dreaded what would meet them when they stepped out into the main chamber. He thought of the Gorm, bursting up from the ground, pouring out into the Munbury longburrow to rip away everything he loved. To see that again, to feel that much terror ... every muscle in his body tried to make him turn and run the other way.

In his hand, Starclaw fizzed and juddered. It was like the dagger knew his fear, and was angry about it. Podkin stared down at it in the gloom. Could it really read his mind? Was it trying to help him?

Anger was good. Anger was powerful. It gave him the courage to keep moving forward down the tunnel, and when he got to the end – well, it might not be enough to make him want to actually *fight* the Gorm, but it would help him find the strength to get past them, if he could. Out into the forest, where he actually stood a chance.

'Quietly now! Keep low!' Crom's commands snapped Podkin from his dreaming, and he realised they were almost at the tunnel mouth.

The other rabbits were all crouched low, keeping to the shadows. Mish jumped on Mash's shoulders to put out a candle that was lighting the tunnel, and it became even darker. They crept forwards, so that they could see into the huge chamber of Boneroot market.

The place was in chaos, but not of the mad, busy, bustling kind. The stalls at the closest end of the market were all overturned and trampled. Goods were crushed and smashed, banners and bunting strewn everywhere. Crowds of jostling rabbits were scrambling away, towards the far end of the chamber, throwing things out of their path as they went. It was a stampede of crazed terror, and Podkin could see what was causing it.

Directly opposite the tunnel mouth they were crouching in was the Boneroot entrance, now crammed full of hunched, armoured shapes. It *was* the Gorm, just as he had known it would be when the alarm sounded.

There were twenty of them at least, standing between the crumbling pillars and winding roots, with more stomping into the chamber behind them.

Torchlight glinted off their cruel armour as they stood in formation, looking around at the place they had just destroyed with their blank red eyes.

'They're just standing there,' whispered Paz. 'Why aren't they chasing the market rabbits?'

Podkin saw she was right. Surely they should be attacking, or at least smashing the rest of the market into pieces? It was almost as if they were waiting for something.

There was a commotion in the tunnel, and Pod realised they were about to find out what. The Gorm parted, making space for someone to enter. Someone taller and fiercer than the rest, with a pair of lopsided iron horns curling upwards from his helmet.

Scramashank.

He was here. He had caught them.

Or had he? Did he know they were hiding, just a few metres away? Maybe the Gorm had just stumbled upon Boneroot by accident? Did that mean they would be able to sneak past and escape somehow?

All these thoughts raced through Podkin's head in a few seconds. He didn't feel brave or angry any more. Even the thrumming dagger he was holding couldn't stop him trembling. He looked up at Crom with white-rimmed, terrified eyes, waiting for the signal to run, run for their lives.

'Hold,' the big rabbit whispered, sensing the fear of the others. 'Not yet. Not yet.'

Podkin grabbed Paz's hand and squeezed tight, looking across at the Gorm and their evil, father-killing lord. There was no sign that he'd seen them. Scramashank was beckoning his troops, two of whom were dragging something down from the entrance.

Was it a rabbit? Yes. A half-dead, beaten scrap of one. By his long beard and patched armour, Podkin recognised him as the guard who had let them in through the hidden door. His face was bruised and bloodied now. He had clearly put up a good fight, for all the good it had done him.

'Lift him up.' Just hearing Scramashank's voice again made Podkin want to cry. Oh, if only he were some kind of legendary warrior, like in the stories, who could storm out there and smash the Gorm to pieces, instead of hiding in a tunnel, trying not to wet himself.

'Can you hear me?' The guard-rabbit had been hoisted upright, and Scramashank was face-to-face with him, staring right into the poor creature's eyes. He made some kind of noise, halfway between a grunt and a whimper.

'Thought you'd hidden yourself away, didn't you? Thought you were all safe from the Gorm, down here in your stinking little pit.'

The rabbit grunted again.

'It was only a matter of time, of course,' Scramashank continued. 'We were bound to find you. Just as we'll find every rabbit in all the Five Realms. There is nowhere you can hide from the Gorm.'

His men cheered at this, and banged their swords against their armour, making a hideous, clanging din that echoed around the chamber. When it had died down, Scramashank grabbed the guard-rabbit's beard and jerked his head up, hard. 'Enough talk. I'm in a good mood today, so I'll give you one chance to spare your miserable life.'

'I'm looking for some rabbits. Little rabbits. A boy, a girl and a baby.'

Podkin and Paz both held their breath, clinging on to each other as hard as they could.

'They have something I want. A dagger or a sword – I'm not sure what it looks like, only that it *isn't* a silver broadsword.' Scramashank paused to snarl, angry that he'd been tricked by Lopkin's decoy. 'If they've been through this festering fleapit, you must have seen them.'

What would the rabbit say? Would he betray them? *Please, please, please*, Podkin thought, not sure who he was even praying to.

The guard-rabbit lifted his head higher with the last of his strength. He opened his mouth to speak, and Scramashank leaned in closer to listen.

Then the brave, wonderful guard spat into the Gorm Lord's face.

There was a moment of total silence that seemed to stretch on forever. Scramashank was like an iron statue, motionless as the gob of spittle ran slowly down the faceplate of his helmet. Then, with a speed and strength that shocked even Podkin, the Gorm Lord grabbed the guard-rabbit and threw him across the chamber.

He sailed through the air like a broken doll, crashing into a candle stall, sending sparks and hot wax showering everywhere. Flames began to spring up amongst the market wreckage and tinder-dry roots, and with nobody to put them out they quickly spread.

Was this the diversion they had been waiting for? Just as Podkin looked up at Crom for a signal, he caught sight of movement from the corner of his eye. The Boneroot rabbits had regrouped themselves into a ragtag army of a kind, and had used the guard's questioning as a diversion. Sneaking up amongst the abandoned stalls, they had crept into position and, even as flames began to leap up around them, they let fly a hail of spears, arrows and stones at the Gorm invaders.

The Battle of Boneroot had started.

Podkin stared on in horror. Besides the attack on Munbury, he had never witnessed any *real* violence, and that had been nothing compared to this. Missiles pinged and zipped through the air, most of them clanging harmlessly off the Gorm armour. A few seconds later, the Gorm responded, sending long, iron-tipped spears whooshing towards the Boneroot rabbits. Around them all, the fire grew, filling the air with stinging smoke.

Still Crom waited.

It wasn't until the flames had spread almost up to the mouth of their tunnel that he finally made a move. Clouds of smoke billowed everywhere. Podkin couldn't even see the Boneroot entrance any more, so he was sure the Gorm couldn't see him.

'*Now*, everybody!' Crom shouted. 'With me, and as fast as you can!'

They stood and ran, down from the tunnel and on to the cavern floor. The entire marketplace had become a bonfire, sending sheets of flame shooting up to the root-covered ceiling above. Showers of sparks whirled amongst the black smoke, and burning streamers of bunting flapped this way and that like huge snakes made of fire. Boneroot rabbits danced in and out of the inferno, shooting arrows then dodging away again before Gorm spears could find them.

'I know a way out,' Crom called back to the group. 'But you must guide me.'

He put out his hand and Podkin grabbed it, thinking to lead him along, but the warrior rabbit hauled him up and on to his back, next to the mewling, shaking Pook.

'Be my eyes, Podkin. We need to find the sellsword stall. Quickly now.'

Podkin had a vague idea where it was, but it was difficult to see in the smoke. He put an arm around Pook to comfort him, then shouted into Crom's ear. 'Forward! Keep going along this side of the cavern!'

With Crom leading the way, and Podkin steering him like a rider on a giant rat, they made their way as quickly as they could along the edge of the market floor. They had to dodge pieces of burning canvas and step through the shattered remains of stalls as they went, which slowed them down dangerously. Podkin snuck a quick glance across the cavern to see the Gorm steadily advancing, stepping through flames that licked off their armour. *I hope they boil inside*, he thought, but they just kept striding on as though they couldn't even feel the heat.

'Nearly there!' he shouted in Crom's ear. He thought he could see the bodies of some rabbits amongst the debris. Was that one of the gambling rabbits, lying curled beneath that broken stall? And there – was that the rabbit with the pickled beetroots that had given them directions when they first arrived? Podkin felt like they should do something, but there was no time to stop and help. It was every rabbit for himself.

'The sellsword market!' Paz yelled. 'There it is!'

Just a few steps further, behind a wall of roiling black smoke; there it was – the fenced enclosure where Podkin had first spotted Crom. He remembered wondering how a blind rabbit could possibly fight. Now his very life depended on him.

'Quick, everyone. Into the enclosure. Head for the stone pillar at the far side. There's a passage behind.'

They all dashed across the now-empty space, past the tattered blanket where Crom had sat for Goddess knows how long. Sure enough, there was a tunnel entrance, just the right size for a small rabbit, hidden amongst the shadows.

Paz was just about to dart in, when something struck the stone pillar by her head with a loud crash. Sharp chips of stone exploded off it, hitting her in the face and knocking her to the floor. It was a spear, Podkin saw, and it had missed spiking her through the head by only a few inches.

Crom spun around, making Pod and Pook cling on for dear life. There, stomping out of the smoke clouds, was a Gorm warrior. His iron armour was blackened by soot, the fur on his ears seared away and the flesh beneath scorched pink. Not that he seemed to care: his jagged broadsword was already swinging towards them, those dead red eyes staring at them as if they were nothing but walking meat.

'Jump back!' Podkin yelled, making Crom leap. Just in time, as the sword *whooshed* past his nose and thudded into the stone floor of the cavern. 'Didn't you hear it coming?'

'The noise,' Crom shouted. 'It's too much. I can't hear where he's coming from. Be my eyes again, Podkin!'

The cacophonic screaming in the cavern, the roar of burning timber, the wash of red-hot air and stink of smoke: all of these things had dulled the senses Crom relied on to make up for his useless eyes.

The Gorm had raised his sword high and was coming at them again.

'Duck!' Podkin screamed. 'Jump right!'

The broadsword swished past them both times, missing them by a few whiskers. How could Crom attack if he couldn't sense the enemy? What if another Gorm came to join in?

'Let's even the field a bit, shall we?' said a voice at Crom's feet.

Podkin looked down to see Mish, her catapult stretched back as far as it would go, pointing at the Gorm's face. Beside her, Mash had the pipe held to his mouth. They both fired at once, little black balls of *something* shooting up at the armoured head of their attacker and hitting both of his helmet's eyeholes at once. The balls exploded, filling the Gorm's eyes with black sticky goo that smoked and burned. The warrior roared, dropping its sword, clawing at its face.

Now was the chance to hit him, but would a blow from Crom be enough to knock him off his feet? There needed to be something behind the warrior's feet – something to make him stumble . . .

A memory popped into Podkin's head from nowhere: playing in the meadows at Midsummer with Rusty and Rufus from Redwater. Pod would creep up behind one and crouch down, and then Paz would push them over, sending them tumbling into the soft, sweet grass. Then they would all roar with laughter, like it was the funniest thing in the world.

A burning underground market was a million miles away from Munbury meadow, but it could still work, couldn't it?

Podkin slipped from Crom's back and dashed around behind the Gorm, crouching into a ball. Paz saw what he was doing, and joined in too, the pair of them making a decent-sized stumbling block.

'Hit him now, Crom!' Podkin shouted. 'Kick out straight ahead of you!'

The warrior rabbit threw himself backwards, dropping to take his weight on his hands and bringing up both feet for a mighty kick. It caught the Gorm in the chest and he toppled, spilling over Podkin and Paz and crashing into one of the stone pillars like a clap of thunder. It was like being rolled over by an iron oak tree, and the two little rabbits were flattened to the hot flagstones, the wind knocked out of them.

Looking up to where the Gorm lay wedged in the pillar, Podkin saw cracks appear in the ancient masonry, and up above there was an ominous groaning sound.

But there wasn't time to worry about that now. Mish and Mash dragged him and Paz up from the floor and the whole group dashed into the tiny burrow, coughing and choking as they went.

*

The tunnel zigged and zagged in all directions and was choked with webs of root and dust. After ten metres or so, it climbed sharply – almost vertically – upwards. There were wooden rungs hammered into the hard earth walls, but many were as old as time, and simply shattered in their grasping hands. Instead, they had to grab fistfuls of roots to haul themselves up.

It was like climbing the inside of a chimney. Cramped, lightless, full of suffocating smoke. They scrabbled as fast as they could, away from the flames and the roaring behind them.

At some point, Pook was knocked from Crom's

back. The big rabbit was on his hands and knees, his shoulders brushing against the tunnel roof. Podkin grabbed him, and with Paz's help, they heaved him up the tunnel between them. Mish and Mash led the way. All of them coughing and choking from the smoke.

Finally, *finally*, they burst out of the darkness and through a mat of overgrown brambles, into the evening light. One by one, they collapsed into the snow at the edge of the forest and lay there, panting and gasping. It was like being born into a new world.

Podkin grabbed great handfuls of snow and mashed it into his face. The smoke had turned his eyes into two throbbing balls of pain, and his nose and throat stung like they had been rubbed with sandpaper and vinegar.

After a few moments, his vision began to return, blurred and watery.

They were well inside the treeline, looking out at the wasteland of shrubs and bushes that hid Boneroot. In the distance, he could make out a shape that might be the stone arch where they had entered. Here and there amongst the trees he could see lines of moving shapes. Streams of rabbits were pouring out of other hidden exits, fleeing their home like ants from a nest that had just been doused with boiling water.

Podkin felt very sorry for them all. They had run from the Gorm to get here, and now they were running again.

'Did you feel that?' Paz said. She was lying beside him, covered head to foot in black soot.

'What?' he croaked.

'The ground. It moved.'

Podkin looked at the forest floor around them, and then he felt it as well. A deep shudder in the bones of the earth.

'The chamber's collapsing,' said Crom. 'We'd better move.'

Even though Crom was right, and their lives were in danger, none of the rabbits had the energy to lift a paw. They sat, coughing and staring, as cracks began to appear in the snow, not ten metres away from them.

With a painful, groaning, ripping sound, the cracks spread. Trees began to lean inwards, and spouts of smoke started seeping from the open wounds in the soil.

'Back!' Crom shouted, and this time they somehow found a last shred of energy – enough to scrabble and drag each other further into the trees where the ground was more solid.

Podkin turned round in time to see a circle the size of the entire Boneroot marketplace tear itself out of the earth, and then everything inside – trees, bushes, mud, snow – all folded downwards into the pit with a crashing roar that shook them off their feet.

Where a messy scrubland had once stood, there was now a gaping hole, oozing black smoke into the darkening sky. On the far side, where the ruined arch still jutted upwards, Podkin could see figures staggering out of the wreck of Boneroot. Armoured, hunched figures, steaming with smoke and burnt blood.

He counted ten, maybe fifteen of them before they stopped coming. Most of the attackers must be buried beneath several tonnes of earth, stone and root below.

Good, he thought, and would have even done a

little dance of joy, had he not spotted the last Gorm soldier to step free of the tunnel.

He was bigger than the rest by a good head, and the spikes on his armour were terrible and huge. White bony things hung from his belt, and he was leaning on a massive two-handed broadsword for support. As Podkin stared, he turned to look across the chasm that Boneroot had left, and Pod was sure he could see two glowing red spots of light in the slits of his helmet.

Podkin felt his lips form the name.

Scramashank. He had survived, Goddess curse him.

'What is it, Pod?' Paz had him by the shoulder and was shaking him, a look of grave worry on her face.

He wanted to answer, but all he could do was point. Paz followed his stare and, when she saw what he had seen, she snatched Pook up into her arms and ran. They all ran, as far and fast into the forest as they could – just as if the devil himself were behind them.

Which, in a way, he was.

Chapter Thirteen

Tales Within Tales

On and on they ran, until it was dark, and the moon was shining down on them like a cold, watchful eye. Eventually they stopped, leaning against tree trunks to rest, and straining to hear above their own rasping and panting – listening for any sounds of clanking armour or cawing of Gorm crows.

'It's freezing out here,' Podkin finally managed to speak. 'But we can't light a fire in case they're following us.'

'And we won't make it through the night if we don't,' said Paz.

'There must be somewhere we can hide,' said Mish.

Mash nodded. 'We could build a shelter from some branches? Or dig a hole in the snow?'

'I know of somewhere we can stay,' said Crom. He heaved himself away from his tree trunk, sniffed the air and started staggering south, deeper into the forest. Pook was snuggled against his chest, having fallen asleep with exhausted terror.

The other rabbits watched him go, half tempted to stay where they were and simply freeze to death until, one by one, they forced themselves to walk after him, into the forest's heart, where the trees were ancient, dark and foreboding.

*

The forest became dense, choked with branches. Thorns and spidery twigs tore at their clothes and sliced their faces. Every now and then, Crom would ask a question about where they were. He was looking for a huge dead oak tree first, then a narrow stream, then a clearing with a ruined log cabin in the centre.

'I don't mean to be rude,' said Podkin, as they

stumbled out of the clearing, still heading southwards, 'but where exactly are we going? We've been walking for hours now. We can't go on much further.' By which he meant that *he* couldn't go on much further, but judging by the gasps and groans the others were making, they were all in a similar state.

As an answer, Crom simply pointed to a large mound they could see rising up amongst the thick trees.

'There,' was all he said, and the rabbits hurried along, not caring what they were rushing to as long as it meant a chance to lie down somewhere dry, warm and safe.

*

The mound was actually a small hill, topped off by a towering scots pine with branches as wide as most other trees' trunks. The great tree sheltered most of the hill from the snow and frosted strands of moss and plants covered everything; ridges and mountains of cracked bark, twining with vines and ivy. The spaghetti-mess of tendrils hung down, trailing over what Podkin first thought was a cave mouth. Looking closer, he saw it was a warren doorway,

set back into the hill and almost swallowed by the growing forest.

'Darkhollow,' Paz said, reading the Ogham runes carved into the stonework. 'I've never heard of it.'

Podkin could make out some time-worn shapes carved into the lichen-covered stone. Some kind of fruit? Pine cones? The wind and rain had smoothed them featureless over many years. This was an old, old warren. Maybe even as ancient as Munbury.

'Nobody's lived here in a long time,' said Mash, thinking the same thing. Mish went up and kicked at the door, making it boom like a drum.

'How are we supposed to get in then?' Podkin asked, through chattering teeth. They all looked at Crom, who silently reached into his jerkin and brought out a long iron key that had been hanging around his neck on a leather thong. The expression on his face was hard to read. Nobody dared speak as he walked up and felt over the surface of the ancient oak door. Finally he found the keyhole and slotted in the key. The lock shrieked, groaned, and then finally clunked. Crom took a deep breath, shoving with his shoulder to open up the entrance.

Cold, musty air hissed out, washing over them in a wave. It smelt of dust and age. They could see nothing inside except a lonely, inky blackness. It was a ghost warren. An empty, lifeless shell of a place.

Crom turned round to face them, spreading his arms wide. 'Welcome to my warren,' he said.

*

The entrance tunnel still had torches sitting in brackets on the wall, as if waiting for someone to return. As the rabbits gingerly stepped over the threshold, Mash took down a torch and lit it with a pair of flints that he kept in a pouch on his belt. When he held the flame high, light filled the burrow, shooting down into the dark depths of the warren, as if the place was hungrily drinking it up.

It looked like it had been deserted for ten, maybe twenty years. Despite the dark, the cold and the shrouds of dust and cobwebs, it had been made well and hadn't leaked or crumbled.

The walls and ceiling were held up by stout wooden beams, all carved with rabbits leaping and twirling through the trunks and roots of the forest.

Pine cones were everywhere, obviously the warren symbol, and in several places Podkin spotted a tall horned rabbit, peering out from a thicket of trees or leaping after a startled weasel. *Hern*, he realised. *The god of the forest.* It made sense that the Darkhollow rabbits would worship him, living in the deepest part of Grimheart itself.

Mash lit more torches from the one in his hand, and other details of the warren appeared. The floor was tiled with patterns and mosaics of coloured clay. There were bare patches on the whitewashed walls, where tapestries had once hung. Wooden doors opened off the main tunnel, on to guards' rooms and weapon stores. In one, they found a stack of torches, lanterns and firewood, all neatly piled, ready for whoever might need it.

They moved into the warren, spreading light as they went. Every now and then someone gasped or made a noise of admiration. It really was a fine place to be hiding out.

Podkin looked behind to see Crom, walking slowly with one hand gently brushing the wall. Was he imagining it, or did the torchlight sparkle on tears in the big rabbit's eyes? Podkin quickly turned away and joined the others in their exploration.

The tunnel led down to the longburrow. Paz and the others dashed about, lighting lanterns and torches, and carrying firewood to stack in the hearth and set alight. It wasn't long before they had a good blaze going, bathing them all in delicious heat and the sweet scent of burning pine. One by one, they collapsed on the tiled floor and stretched out, letting the warmth ease their aches and pains. Podkin couldn't describe how good it felt to be in a proper warren again, safe and warm in the bones of the earth.

They all sat in silence for a while, looking round at their new home.

It had clearly been a wealthy warren. The fireplace was carved stone, and there were long feasting tables and hundreds of wooden chairs, all with a little pine cone carved into the back, all sitting quietly in the dark, waiting for the next feast to begin.

The warren tapestries were rolled and stacked in a corner. Mash unfurled one and held it up to show the tall horned rabbit again, this time standing next to a stag whose neck was garlanded with pine cones.

It reminded Podkin of Munbury: an orderly, tidy, pretty little warren that had once seemed like the centre of the world. Except Darkhollow was so empty and lost. It was lonely – a sad, hidden thing, sleeping and dreaming away the years until life and light returned.

It took a while for them all to finish warming up and calming down. Smoke still stung eyes and chests, and everyone was smudged black with soot and mud. Only their feet, which had crunched through miles of snow on their way here, were clean. Brown, white and grey toes wiggled by the fire, slowly coming back to life.

'Are we safe here?' Podkin had to ask. 'Will the Gorm find us?'

Crom rubbed at his tired eyes for a moment before answering. 'I don't think they will. The pine trees are too thick for their crows and their armour. And if they follow anyone from Boneroot, it'll be all the other rabbits. They left much more of a trail than we did.'

Podkin wondered if it was right to feel so relieved that rabbits other than him would be hunted down in his place. But it was difficult not to.

The others must have been thinking the same uncomfortable thoughts. As a distraction, they started giving each other looks, seeing who would be brave enough to ask Crom his story. In the end, it was Mish who spoke up, her little voice echoing about the empty hall.

'Why is this place so empty, Crom?' she asked.

The blind rabbit sat still and silent for so long, Podkin wondered whether he had heard the question. When he spoke, his words were heavy and tired, as if it was a story he didn't want to tell.

*

'I don't suppose you can imagine me as a young rabbit – maybe a few years older than yourselves – but I was once. That was when I first met your father, Podkin.

'The custom in those days was for the sons of chieftains to be sent to live with other clans. Ones where there was a chance of fighting going on, so as to teach them a bit about being a leader and a warrior. Otherwise it was easy for rabbits to become spoilt and lazy. And spoilt, lazy rabbits make bad rulers.' Paz gave Podkin a *very* pointed look. He stuck his tongue out at her.

'Well,' Crom continued. 'Your father was son of a chief, and so was I. This was my father's warren, and I was due to take over from him.

'As it was, Lopkin and I were sent to a warren called Flintchip, up north in the shadow of the Arukh mountains. They were having problems with long-haired Arukh rabbits and needed men to fight them.

'So fighting was what Lopkin and I did.

'At first I didn't know what I was doing. I had spent all my life lying around in meadows, nibbling clover and snoozing. I hid away from my weapon teachers and couldn't even read or write. I only just about knew one end of a sword from the other.'

That doesn't sound so bad, Podkin thought. He made sure he ignored Paz, who was sniggering and pointing at him.

'So when it came to my first actual battle, I very nearly died.

'I don't know if you've seen the Arukh rabbits.

They are fierce, screaming warriors, with long manes of hair that they braid and hang with beads and paint bright blue. They fight with stone weapons, but they are deadly and well-trained warriors.

'Your father and I were arrow-boys when our army marched on them. All we had to do was keep the archers supplied with fresh arrows and stay well out of the fighting.

'But things didn't go to plan, and a bunch of Arukhs broke through the line. They managed to get as far as the archers, and knocked several of them down. One big Arukh buck smashed right through to where I was positioned, and was about to bring his stone axe down on my head. I just stood there, staring up at him in surprise.

'Then your father, who was no bigger than you are now, leapt up at him, grabbed hold of his braids and smashed him over the head with a clay bottle. Knocked him out cold. Eight summers' old, and able to take down an Arukh warrior. That was your father.'

Podkin and Paz looked at each other. Both had tears in their eyes, but they managed to share a smile.

'After that, I vowed to make a soldier of myself.

Lopkin and I trained every day, and a year or two later we were on the front lines with the rest of the warriors. Proper little scrappers we were, and the life of a soldier started to suit us.

'So much so, that once the Arukhs had been tamed, we carried on looking for adventure. The two of us travelled over most of the Five Realms, helping out wherever there was trouble. We were together every day for five or six years, and we saved each others' lives so many times that I lost count.

'Then one day, word came to Lopkin that his father, your grandfather, had died, and that it was time for him to return home and rule the warren. He was pleased to go, even though it was hard for us to say goodbye. I think, in his heart, he had finally grown tired of the warrior life.

'I hadn't, though. Far from it. I kept on travelling and fighting. I stopped by Munbury once, just after Lopkin was married. Your mother was a fine rabbit, and he was happy. That was when he showed me the dagger, and told me about how it was one of the Twelve.

'I didn't stop for long, as there was more action to

be had. Fighting the giant rabbits in Orestad, pushing back the cult of Cruach, the war god in Thrianta. Then, one day, word came to me that *my* father had passed away, and it was time to come back to Darkhollow and rule as he had.

'I thought long and hard about it, but in the end I refused. I knew what it would mean for the rabbits living here, but I just couldn't give up the life of a soldier. Being a chieftain – it just wasn't in me. I thought the Darkhollow rabbits would choose someone else, but instead they just moved on. Some to Inkcap Dell in the north, some to Stumphaven down south. Others headed off to Orestad. Formed a warren of their own in the forest there, last I heard. They always were a stubborn, superstitious lot. They'd rather start afresh somewhere new than carry on in a place they thought had run out of luck. And the warren has sat here empty ever since.'

The rabbits sat for a while, thinking about Crom's story, listening to the crackle of the fire. They had heard about warrens being taken over by the Gorm, or being wiped out in some tribal war or other, but they had never imagined a whole tribe giving up and moving on.

Maybe they had never been happy at Darkhollow in the first place. Or, more likely, losing their chieftain had been seen as some kind of sign from the gods. Religion made rabbits do some very strange things, sometimes.

Finally, Podkin spoke up with another question. 'What about your eyes, Crom? How did you go blind? If you don't mind me asking, that is.'

Crom made a noise that was part sigh, part growl. Podkin thought he wasn't going to tell them, but then he spoke again.

'That was five years or more ago. When the Gorm appeared, up north. Some warrens put together a party to go and scare them off, but we weren't prepared for them. Our spears just bounced off their armour, off those twisted monsters they ride ...

'And there was something else – a witch-rabbit. She rode a black rat and called down lightning from the sky. We charged on her, but she caught me full in the face with a bolt of thunder. Her magic took my sight, and I lay under a pile of bodies for days in some kind of trance. When I woke up, the Gorm were gone, marching on another poor warren somewhere. I crawled away, helpless as a baby. I could tell the land all around was burnt and blackened – it was poisoned and stank of iron and blood. Luckily some rabbits fleeing the Gorm army found me. They took me with them and healed my wounds, but they couldn't do anything about my eyes.

'In the years since then, I've taught myself to fight again, how to use my other senses to get by. But I'll never be the warrior I once was. I used to wish that the Gorm witch had killed me, but now I'm glad to be alive. When you lose something as precious as your sight, you learn to appreciate everything else more.'

With the stories finished, and Pook already snoring his little head off, the rest of the rabbits began to curl up in their cloaks to fall asleep. There were probably beds and blankets somewhere in the darkness of the empty warren, but rooting around to find them was too much effort.

Podkin snuggled up with his back to Paz, enjoying the heat of the fire on his face and the scar of his missing ear. It was like being stroked softly to sleep by an old friend.

His last sight, before his eyes closed, was of Crom, sitting silently in the firelight.

Podkin imagined him as a young rabbit, standing next to his father, laughing and joking together, all those years ago. Then, with his dreams as warm as his toes, he fell fast asleep.

*

The first few weeks in the empty warren were a peaceful time. They spent their days exploring the tunnels, lighting and airing the dusty old rooms and foraging in the forest above for nuts and berries to eat.

Evenings were spent huddled by the great hearth in the longburrow, and what had started with Crom's tale became a kind of storytelling tradition, for firesides and stories share a special kind of magic together.

They heard all about the life of Mish and Mash and their acrobat troupe. They had joined it when the travelling caravan visited their little village in the Eiskalt mountains.

The dwarf rabbits there lived in warrens carved into the cliffs and were expert rock and tree climbers before they could walk. But Mish and Mash had longed to see the world, and the troupe was a perfect place for them to show off their acrobatic skills. (This part of the story was embellished with exhibitions of several backflips, headstands and feats of balancing that had the little rabbits whooping with applause.)

The dwarf rabbits travelled all over Thrianta and Hulstland in the south, with their band of jugglers, fire-breathers and puppeteers. Life was pleasant and easy then, until they came over the Razorback downs into Enderby.

That was when they first came across the Gorm. The warren where they were performing was raided, and some of their troupe were taken as slaves.

After that, they became something more than just acrobats. They found ways to use their skills to bring down the armoured Gorm giants, and if they met a patrol on their travels, then they made sure there were two or three Gorm who didn't return home to base.

Mish and Mash paused to show the others the contents of their bandoliers. They were full of little packets: mixtures they had made to fire at the cracks and gaps in Gorm armour. There was blinding goo (which everyone had already seen), poison, glue, itching powder, stink bombs and something called 'bang dust'. Everyone was suitably impressed.

So, returning to the story, Mish and Mash and their troupe of guerrilla Gorm fighters still travelled from warren to warren, staying ahead of the Gorm and helping where they could.

Boneroot was a natural place for them to end up, full as it was of refugees and runaways. They had paused there to resupply and to make a few copper coins from performing when the two dwarf rabbits had been snatched from their lodgings by the evil Quince and Shape, and hidden away until their troupe gave up looking for them. When Mish was finally let out on a stealing expedition, they were nowhere to be found.

And the rest of the story, everyone knew very well.

Paz and Podkin took turns telling the tale of their epic escape from the Gorm, and how Podkin lost his ear. After that, there were more stories about life in Munbury warren before everything went so horribly wrong. They talked about Midsummer parties at the standing stones, the time Paz pushed Podkin into the river; Bramblemas Eves, waiting for the Midwinter Rabbit, games of hide-and-seek in the forest . . .

At first, Podkin almost couldn't bear talking about happier times, knowing they were gone forever. But once he began to share his previous life with his new friends, it gave him a kind of comfort. Those memories were like precious, perfect jewels that he would treasure and keep with him forever.

Darkhollow warren was bleak and empty and buried in the forest, but it was also safe and secret and, by night, full of laughter and the crackle of firewood. Little by little, the rabbits began to think of it as home.

INTERLUDE

T he bard pauses, takes a swig from his cup.

'Is that it?' says the inquisitive rabbit, folding her arms and pouting. 'What about when Podkin becomes the Horned King? What about all the battles and fighting and chopping things into pieces with his magic dagger?'

'This must be when he starts to be the Horned King,' says the sensible rabbit. 'The warren in the forest is where his army lives in the stories. They have a secret home where nobody can find them, don't they?'

'That's just stupid,' replies the inquisitive rabbit. 'Why would a whole warren full of rabbits just up and leave? If your dad vanished, we'd just pick another chieftain, and carry on like before.'

There is a grunt from the fireside, where Chief Hubert has been listening along. The inquisitive rabbit has the decency to squirm and look embarrassed.

'The way rabbits feel about their chieftains is complicated,' says the bard. 'They believe they are chosen by the Goddess herself to lead them. If a warren loses its chief, and he has no sons to take over, it is seen as a bad omen. So they would often rather pack up and find homes elsewhere, in happy, lucky warrens.'

'So Darkhollow is cursed?' the sensible rabbit asks.

'Perhaps,' says the bard. 'But then, its chief did come back, in a way. And besides, not everyone believes in all that rubbish.'

'Never mind that,' says the inquisitive rabbit. 'What about the fighting? When does Podkin One-Ear get revenge against the Gorm?'

'Stories aren't all about fighting and revenge,' says the bard. 'You have to have a bit of character development in there as well. Some suspense, some atmosphere. A little bit of romance.'

'Yuck!' All the listening rabbits make retching,

spewing noises and pull their ears over their eyes. The bard sighs.

'By Clarion's sacred harp strings, you lot are a hard crowd to please,' he says. 'Very well. Revenge against the Gorm it is then.'

CHAPTER FOURTEEN

The Wagon in the Woods

A month or so passed in the warren of Darkhollow, and everyone had fallen into a comfortable routine.

The warren had been thoroughly swept and aired – dust sheets removed, cobwebs brushed away. The place looked more like a home and less of a haunted shell. The rabbits had found their own rooms amongst the empty burrows, beaten and plumped the mattresses and settled themselves in. Mish and Mash were bunked next door to Podkin, Paz and Pook, and Crom had chosen a room on the other side of the longburrow. Podkin had thought Crom might take the old chieftain's chambers, but he had opted for a simple cell with a cot and a rack for his armour and weapons. Nobody questioned him about his choice.

The short winter days were spent keeping busy. Mornings saw Podkin, Paz and Pook foraging the forest floor for winter caches of nuts and seeds hidden away by squirrels. Mish and Mash took to the trees, gathering whatever they could find, while Crom chopped firewood.

In the afternoon, the rabbits trained. Mish and Mash taught the little ones acrobatics – backflips, headstands and somersaults – and Crom gave Podkin sword lessons. The little rabbit was a bit reluctant at first, but Crom insisted that a chieftain's son *must* know how to fight. And there was no sneaking off to a hidden cupboard or secret cubbyhole this time. Crom was nothing like old Melfry, the weaponmaster from Munbury. Every time he got even slightly cross with Podkin, the image of Shape and Quince getting pummelled flashed through the little rabbit's mind. Crom was not someone you wanted to annoy.

They used wooden practice swords, which,

Podkin quickly discovered, tended to leave nasty welts and bruises wherever they hit you (which was pretty much everywhere). Paz usually joined the classes as well, much to Podkin's annoyance. She stood nearby, mirroring his movements with her own sword. From the corner of his eye, Podkin could see she was naturally much better than him, which only made him angry. *That* made him lose his focus and make mistakes, leading to another clonk on the head.

Sometimes Crom asked her to join in, and that was even more embarrassing. Paz was bigger, quicker and faster than Pod, and it was all he could do to keep dodging and rolling out of the way. He wished she'd go and play with Pook or hunt berries for tea.

One afternoon in particular was really difficult for Podkin. He had been working on blocking and parrying with Crom, and for once felt like he was getting somewhere. After he had managed to turn aside Crom's wooden blade for the third time, they paused for a breather. As Pod leant on his sword, panting for breath and rubbing the latest lump on his head, Crom cleared his throat.

Thinking that he was due some praise for his effort, Podkin's little chest puffed up and a smile twitched the corners of his mouth. A good word from Crom had come to mean so much to the little rabbit, especially as it didn't happen very often.

But instead, the old warrior waved a hand at where Paz was standing, swishing her sword about and generally showing off. 'Come on, Paz. Let's see if he can block you as well.'

Oh, badgers' bottoms, thought Podkin, as his sister came skipping over, cocky as anything and grinning from ear to ear. Before he could protest, she swung her wooden sword at him, just missing his whiskers.

'Don't dodge, Podkin. Block!'

Jab, jab, swing. Paz came at him relentlessly. He tried to remember the parrying technique he'd just mastered, but in his panic not to let his sister beat him, it all went out of his head.

Clonk! She caught him on the shoulder. *Whack!* She smacked him on his nose. She was winding up for another swing, when Pod's temper got the better of him.

'Stop it!' he screamed, and flung his practice

sword at Paz. 'This is stupid! I'm never going to learn to fight! I don't *want* to learn to fight! Paz can be the chieftain, and she can stick her poxy wooden swords in her earholes!'

Crom's brow was furrowed; Paz's face was surprised and worse, amused. He'd made a complete idiot of himself in front of his father's old friend, just like the old, spoilt Podkin would have done. It was too much. He turned and ran off into the woods.

An hour or so later, when he couldn't feel his toes any more, he slunk back into the warren. Crom was waiting for him by the fire. Podkin went and stood before him, shivering. He expected a telling-off – deserved it, even. He knew that.

But Crom just put one of his big scarred hands on Podkin's shoulder and gently squeezed.

'I'm sorry,' Podkin said, his voice small and almost lost amongst the crackling of the fire.

'Don't be,' said Crom. 'You did well today. I shouldn't have pushed you so hard. I forget how young you are, sometimes. Goddess knows, you should have seen me when I was your age. I didn't know a spear from a carrot.'

'But Paz . . .'

'She's older and bigger than you. Her reach is longer, and she's fast. But keep trying like you did today and you'll be the one whacking her on the head soon enough.'

That will make a nice change, thought Podkin, but didn't say it aloud. Instead he promised himself he wouldn't lose his cool again. He wanted to make Crom proud, maybe because it was the closest he could get to making his father proud. And from then on he doubled his effort, swallowed his pride and tried to learn something from each new bruise.

In the evenings they prepared whatever they had scavenged from the forest and sat down to eat by the fire. There was never very much, and their stomachs always seemed empty, but at least they didn't starve. The Darkhollow well was still good and, with a supply of fresh water, Crom thought they would be fine until the spring when there would be more food around. (Podkin was very glad, because the warrior rabbit had told them several stories about being stranded with no food and having to eat worms and beetles. Pook seemed quite excited by the idea, but the only crunchy things Podkin liked to eat were carrots and turnips.)

And that was how life went on: pleasantly boring and quiet. Up until, that is, the day that Mish and Mash saw the wagon.

*

They had been in the top branches of a pine tree, Mash told them later, when they heard the squeaking of wagon wheels. Having grown up travelling the Five Realms by wagon, they would have known the sound anywhere.

Seeing as they hadn't met a soul since stepping into the forest nearly two months ago, they were very curious about whom it could be. Clambering and flipping from tree to tree, they followed the sound until they were looking down at a rough, narrow track that wound between the trees.

Wobbling along the rutted road was an old wagon, pulled by a mangy, exhausted creature with matted fur. It might have been a giant rat, but it looked more like a walking skeleton with a broken, stumpy tail and torn, flea-bitten ears.

There were two rabbits sitting on the driving

board, one with a hooked spear, which he used to jab the rat every now and then. The creature was too exhausted even to squeal. It just plodded slightly faster for a few seconds, until the next spiking came its way.

The wagon itself was filled with supplies. They spotted sacks of grain and oats, reed baskets of potatoes and beetroot and kegs marked with the sign of Silverock warren. That could mean only one thing: that gallons of famous Silverock mead would be sloshing around inside.

This instantly got the two dwarf rabbits' stomachs rumbling, and they whispered about whether to try and hook a barrel off the wagon. They also thought about following it, but weren't sure they could find their way back again. Not wanting to end up lost and alone in the deep dark forest, they set off to Darkhollow to report back.

That night, they all sat by the fire and wondered about the wagon and where it might have been going.

'It can't be Boneroot,' said Podkin. 'The warren has completely collapsed. Wasn't it the only place north of here for miles and miles?'

Crom shook his head. 'There's Applecross

warren, up by the river. But trade for them won't come through this part of the forest. It goes upriver on narrow boats.'

'What's wrong with this part of the forest?' Paz asked.

'It's haunted, of course,' Crom smiled. 'There's a cursed warren of ghost rabbits here, didn't you know? That and the Beast of Grimheart.'

'The Beast of what?' Podkin said. 'You never told us there was a beast running around here! We've been walking around the forest every day for ages now!'

'Relax,' said Crom. 'I lived here for years and never saw it. It's just an old legend. In fact, I'm pretty sure we made it up ourselves, just to keep visitors away. The Darkhollow rabbits always were an antisocial bunch.'

'So where can the wagon be going then?' Mish asked. 'Do you think we could rob it?'

'Robbing is theft, and that is wrong,' said Crom. 'But let us keep an ear out for it. If it comes again, we will follow and find out where it's headed.'

*

It snowed harder than ever for the next two weeks: hard enough for drifts to break through the dense branches of the tree canopy and to cover the forest floor. It made foraging nearly impossible, and the rabbits were hungrier than ever. Tracking the cart was the last thing on their minds but, once the snow had eased off and the forest road thawed a bit, Mish and Mash started keeping an ear out again.

One morning they came rushing into the clearing outside Darkhollow, where Crom was busy chopping wood.

'We heard it!' they cried. 'The cart is back! It's just gone past us, heading north again.'

Moments later, Podkin, Paz and the two dwarf rabbits were at the roadside, following the fresh tracks of the cart and rat. (Pook was too small for this adventure and had been left safely behind with Crom, who insisted he was too clumsy to be crashing his way around the woods by touch, when stealth and creeping was called for.)

The rabbits hung back far enough to be hidden from the cartsmen, but close enough to hear the wagon squeaking and the snow crunching under the giant rat's paws. To find their way back again, they carved crosses into tree trunks here and there, for it was a long cold walk out of the forest.

At last they reached the edge and could spy the cart in the distance. Keeping far back and low to the ground, they followed its marks through the pristine snow. For an hour or more they trudged along, thinking it might never stop, when the track disappeared over the brow of a small hill.

When the rabbits caught up, they lay on the ground and peered down into the valley. If their blood hadn't already been close to ice, what they saw would have made it run cold.

Down below was a cluster of tents, dusted with snow and ringed by a palisade of wooden stakes. The cart was rolling towards it, and coming out to meet it were several rabbits. Large rabbits. Large *armoured* rabbits.

'It's a Gorm camp!' Podkin hissed. Every rabbit instinct in his body told him to turn and run and not stop until he was deep in the forest, locked away inside his new warren. Instead he bit back the fear, like he had in Boneroot, letting burning anger take its place.

'What are they doing here?' Paz whispered. 'I thought they lived in Splinterholm, far up in the north?'

'They do,' Mash agreed. 'But there must be lots of warrens around here to control. Maybe this is the base they do it from.'

Podkin thought about all the places nearby that had fallen under Gorm control. There was Redwater, and Munbury of course. Further north, by the lakeside, were Applecross and Cherrywood, and probably more that he hadn't heard of. They would need somewhere nearby for all that conquering and pillaging.

He peered closer at the camp, trying to count how many Gorm there might be. At least twenty, he thought – maybe more in those tents. And lots of other rabbits besides. Servants and slaves, probably. But what about those ones in the corner of the camp? Were they shut in some kind of enclosure or something?

'Prisoners,' he said, under his breath. The others looked at him.

'What was that, Pod?' Paz asked.

'Prisoners,' he said. 'Down in the corner there. It looks like they've got people cooped up. Paz, what if . . . ?'

He didn't need to say it. Both of them had kept a secret hope, ever since leaving Munbury, that their mother and aunt might still be alive. Neither of them had mentioned it, in case speaking it aloud might break it or make it vanish, but now, with what lay down in the valley below them . . .

'Can you see her?' Paz asked, craning her neck.

'Not yet, but maybe . . . if we could get closer . . .'

'Keep down!' Mash grabbed the two rabbits by their cloaks and pulled them down into the snow. 'You're going to give us away.'

'But what if . . .' Podkin said. 'We have to . . .'

'We *have* to get back to Crom,' said Mish. 'He needs to know about this. Maybe he can come up with a plan.'

Podkin knew that was right but he couldn't pull himself away, not if his mother might still be down there. In the end it was Paz who made him leave, taking him by the hand and gently pulling him, all the while staring him in the eyes with a look that told him they would be back. Absolutely, definitely, they would be back.

*

'There's no way you're going back,' said Crom. He had folded his arms and was looking as stern as possible (which was actually pretty stern). 'Twenty Gorm? It would be suicide.'

'But we'd have *you* with us,' Podkin said. They were all sat by the fire after a paltry dinner of acorn bread and dried mushrooms.

'Doesn't matter,' said Crom. 'I could take out one, maybe two at best. That still leaves eighteen. Are you going to take on eighteen Gorm? With your magical dagger that can't even cut through their armour?'

'We could try,' said Paz. 'We might be able to come up with some kind of plan. We have to do *something.*'

'You don't even know that your mother is there,' said Crom. 'It's not worth the risk. I know how you feel ... I've lost people before ... but you'd only end up being caught yourselves. Or killed, even. Would your mother want that?'

238

There was nothing that could be said. Mish and Mash had already headed off to their beds, exhausted by the long walk through the snow. Pook was quietly snoring in Paz's arms, so Paz and Podkin lit a candle and took him off to their room, leaving Crom to sit and listen to the snaps and crackles of the fire alone.

Podkin waited until the door was firmly shut, and Pook tucked into his little cot in the corner of their tiny room. He set the candle on the shelf between his and Paz's beds and watched as it cast dancing shadows over the earthen walls.

'Well?' he said. 'Do you reckon we could do it without him?'

Paz started to sigh, but in the end it came out as more of a sob. 'Pod, we couldn't even do it *with* him. He's right. We'd just be handing ourselves over to the Gorm.' She sat down on her bed and hugged herself, looking sad and very tired.

'So we're just going to sit here and let them kill our mother too? Or turn her into some kind of slave?'

'We don't even know if she's there, Podkin. We didn't see her, did we? She could be back in Munbury warren, looking after the place like ... like ...'

She didn't have to say it. Podkin knew what she meant. *Like Lady Russet.* A hollow-eyed zombie, running her own warren for her new masters. The thought of that woman made Podkin's missing ear give a ghostly twitch. Could that be right? Was there an ugly metal pillar in the middle of Munbury longburrow, watching as Pod's old friends and family cowered before the Gorm? Had their beautiful childhood home become a dead, evil place like Redwater?

'No,' he said. 'No. We talked about that, don't you remember? In the snow burrow, that night before Boneroot. You said mother would never do that. You even laughed at the idea.'

'I know I did, Pod.' Paz sob-sighed again. 'But maybe I was wrong. Or maybe she managed to escape – get clear away from Munbury and the Gorm. Or she might have told them where to go and they could have ...' She couldn't bear to finish that thought. She hugged herself tighter, trying to make her brother understand.

'The point is, we have no idea *where* she could be. And we don't have any way to find out. Not unless we want to charge into a Gorm camp and end up as a bunch of skulls dangling from Scramashank's belt.'

Podkin sat and stared at his sister for a while. She was right, of course (why was she *always* right?) and so was Crom, but it didn't make it any easier. He couldn't understand why they were both so ready to just give up. Was that something that happened to you when you got older? You grew up, became sensible and gave up hoping for anything?

'I *know* she's there,' he said, eventually, in a quiet voice. And in saying it, he realised that he *did* actually know. Somewhere inside him – in his heart, maybe – there was a hard little nugget of certainty. He *knew* his mother was in that camp as surely as he knew carrots were orange.

'You don't really, Pod.'

'I do. By the Goddess's curly whiskers, I do. And I'm not just saying it to be difficult, Paz. Not this time. I swear to you she's there, and we have to save her. Her and all those other poor prisoners. You have to trust me on this. Please.'

Paz stared at him long and hard, her eyes glinting

in the candlelight. Finally she shrugged and flicked her ears at him.

'Fine. If you can come up with a plan that can beat twenty Gorm, I'll be right there with you. And it'd better be a good plan, mind. One that doesn't end up with us all getting skinned. Goodnight, Podkin.'

And with that, she blew out the candle and snuggled down in her bed, leaving Podkin staring at a dark ceiling.

Twenty Gorm. He couldn't rescue his mother because there were twenty Gorm in the way. He couldn't fight them; he couldn't outrun them. What did he have that could get rid of them without getting himself or his friends killed?

It came to him in the last few seconds of wakefulness, just as he teetered on the edge of sleep. He never knew if it was a dream, an idea of his own, or a special thought sent into his head when he most needed it. It was important, though, and he clung to it all night, so it wouldn't be lost come the morning.

He had two things that would help him beat twenty Gorm: he knew where their food came from and, most importantly, he was friends with a witch.

CHAPTER FIFTEEN

The Battle of Camp Gorm

It took Podkin several days to convince Crom that his plan would work, and then several more for them to find Brigid's house again. They knew she was somewhere west of Boneroot, along the outskirts of Grimheart forest, but he had been in no fit state to take much notice when he was last there.

So they had to set out on daily expeditions, marking the trees as they went, heading further and further outwards. Eventually they went so far that they had to camp out overnight in another snow burrow, but were rewarded the next day when they stood before a huge gnarled oak that looked a little familiar.

'Could this be it?' Podkin said to Paz. She shrugged, looking over to where a bored Mish and Mash were doing backflips in the snow.

'Well, don't just stand around on the doorstep,' came a voice from deep in the woods. 'Walk up and give the door a knock.'

Mish and Mash both squealed in shock and landed flat on their faces. Podkin and Paz were less surprised when a cloaked figure stepped out from among the trees. Brigid had been there all along.

She watched Mish and Mash pick themselves up from the floor with her blue eyes twinkling. Podkin thought they looked much brighter than usual. Brigid's face also seemed less lined, her back not so stooped.

'Not very agile for acrobats, are they?' she said.

'How did she—' Mish began.

'Know that?' Brigid interrupted. 'I know lots of things, dearie. Come on inside. I've got that potion Podkin's about to ask me for.'

With Mish and Mash staring as though their

eyes were about to pop out of their heads, they all sat around Brigid's fire and shared a pot of stinging-nettle tea. She had mixed something up in a leather pouch, which she gave to Podkin. He slipped it into his belt with a nod. 'For sweet dreams?' he asked, just to check. Brigid winked.

'And also,' she added, 'I've got that thing you two acrobats were after as well. "Bang dust", don't you call it?'

Mish and Mash gaped. They had only had the idea of using the explosive powder that very morning and hadn't even told Podkin yet. Brigid went over to one of her cupboards and brought out two little barrels, one for each of the dwarf rabbits.

'Stinky stuff,' said Brigid. 'Mixed it up a few months ago. Had to call in a few favours from an old friend of mine to get the sulphur and saltpetre. I hope you two know what you're doing with it.'

It was Podkin and Paz's turn to look surprised, but before they could say anything, Brigid took them both by the hand.

'There's one more thing,' she said. 'I'm going to be coming with you.'

'Back to Darkhollow?' Podkin said.

Brigid waggled her ears. 'Yes, but also on this little expedition of yours. You're going to need me.'

'You can't do that!' Paz cried. 'It's too dangerous.'

'Oh, I can take care of myself,' Brigid smiled. 'Especially lately. I've been growing stronger and stronger every day.'

Podkin was about to ask what she was talking about, but Paz already had an idea. 'Because of the Balance you told us about? The picture of the snake?'

'Yes, dear. Very good.' Brigid patted Paz on the head as if she were a clever student. 'The Gorm have been growing far too powerful. The Balance doesn't like that. It's beginning to swing the other way. And I plan to help it.'

Podkin wasn't sure what that meant, but it couldn't be denied that she looked like a new rabbit. And even though he didn't want to put Brigid in danger, the thought of having her along made him feel much better about their chances.

*

The next part was much trickier.

With Mish and Mash both on watch for the

Gorm's supply wagon, it wasn't long before it was spotted again. Wobbling along the rutted, snowy track with its weary guards and exhausted rat, the rabbits managed to sneak along behind it, hiding in the snowdrifts and undergrowth.

Further up the track, Podkin had used Starclaw to slice down a small tree and topple it across the path, creating a simple roadblock.

When the guards stopped the wagon and climbed down to chop the tree out of the way, Podkin and Mash slipped aboard.

Luckily, the sound of hacking wood masked any noise they made as they swiftly added Brigid's mixture to all the sacks of wheat and grain. They poured it into the mead barrels and sprinkled it over the loaves of bread, until everything in the cart had a good dose. All the while, Paz and Mish kept watch, until the guards had almost finished clearing the tree. Then Paz gave a little whistle and the sneaking rabbits hopped down from the wagon and into the bushes.

The guards carried on their way, completely unaware that their cargo had been tampered with.

'Tonight, then,' Paz said, when they were gone.

'Yes,' said Podkin. 'Tonight.' His fur bristled with electric tingles at the thought.

*

It was a full moon with a clear sky, and the stars were spectacular. Podkin could see the Big Radish, Clarion the Bard and the Goddess herself: all the constellations gleaming amongst clouds of trillions upon trillions of twinkling lights. He wondered whether some rabbit had taken the time to name all of them, and if perhaps he should have spent a bit more time studying astronomy instead of sneaking off for naps and games of tag.

The silver glow reflected off the snow all around and glinted in tiny sparkles, like a mirror for the stars.

He sat with Paz, Mish, Mash and Crom. Brigid was there too, with Pook curled up asleep in a papoose under her cloak. They couldn't have left him behind on his own in Darkhollow, and Brigid had promised to stay back, out of the camp and the action (although Podkin had spotted the twinkle in her eye as she said it, and he wondered whether she really would).

Together, they all perched on the brow of the hill, looking down at the Gorm camp. They had wrapped themselves in white woollen blankets for camouflage and looked like harmless lumps of snow. But underneath they were clad in leather armour from Darkhollow, and armed with daggers, swords and clubs. Mish and Mash also clutched the small wooden barrels that Brigid had given them, although they had still not told anyone else what they planned to do with it.

Crom had emerged from his father's old chambers looking especially impressive. He wore a suit of lacquered scale armour, made from toughened, painted layers of leather, and he carried a long shield, a sword and an ash spear. Podkin had wondered if it might be a magic weapon, like his own father's dagger, but Crom had just shaken his head. If there was a sacred treasure in Darkhollow, that wasn't it.

They all sat in silence, apart from Pook's gentle snoring, looking down on the enemy rabbits who were finishing their dinner. The Gorm were sitting around a fire inside the camp fences. Behind them was a cook's bench. They had all been tucking into bowls of stew and loaves of bread. If their plan had worked, Brigid's concoction should start taking effect any minute now.

Podkin held his breath and waited some more.

The Gorm sat motionless around the fire. None of them moved or even seemed to speak. Surely the sleep potion should have started working by now? *Come on*, Podkin urged. *Fall over. Have a lovely evening snooze.*

As if they had heard his silent wish, one of the Gorm wobbled. He swayed forwards, backwards, and then – like an enormous iron tree being toppled – keeled over into the snow face first.

None of the others moved or even reacted.

Then, just as if a giant row of dominoes had been knocked over, they all began to topple, crashing to the ground and lying there, half covered in frost and snoring like babies.

'It worked!' Paz whispered. 'Podkin, you're a genius! And you too, Brigid!'

'Don't count your carrots before they're grown,' said Brigid. 'You're not even in the camp yet.'

'Give it a few more moments,' said Crom. 'Then we go down.'

*

The walk down to the camp was a terrifying one. They left Brigid and Pook on the hillside and began to crunch their way through the thick snow. Podkin expected a hail of spears or arrows to come down on their heads at any second; they were entering the very heart of the Gorm stronghold and there would be no way for them to escape.

But nothing came flying over the wooden fence, and Podkin and the others soon stood by the gates, an eerie silence all around. Using Starclaw, Podkin sliced a hole through the middle of the doors, chopping out the latch on the other side. He pushed the wooden circle through, and it fell with a thud on to the frozen snow inside the camp.

'Well,' he said. 'That was incredibly easy.'

'Carrots. Counting,' Paz reminded him.

Crom pushed open one of the gates, and they walked inside the camp. They almost stumbled over two sleeping Gorm. Up close the iron-clad warriors looked even more terrifying. It was only their loud snoring that gave Podkin the confidence to carry on – that, and the thought that his mother might be somewhere nearby.

There were tents to the left and right of them, but all seemed to be empty. The atmosphere was quiet and peaceful. Tranquil, almost, if it wasn't for the shivers of pure terror jangling about in Podkin's blood.

The enormous fire at the centre of the camp cast fingers of orange light across the snow, and sparkled on the mounds of dozing iron that were the unconscious Gorm. *I forgot to ask how long they would be asleep*, Podkin thought, with a twinge of worry. *It must be long enough for us to get in and out, or Brigid wouldn't have let us come. Would she?*

In any case, he hurried his footsteps, tiptoeing past the sleeping soldiers, heading for the prisoners' pen on the far side.

Until, that is, something brought him to a sudden stop.

There, sticking up out of the snowy ground like a rotting, poisonous tooth, was a hunk of metal.

A gigantic warped shard of rusted, pitted iron. It reminded Podkin of the statue-like shard they'd seen in the middle of Redwater longburrow, but this one was much, much bigger. It was studded with serrated spikes and jagged nodules, like warts on a toad's back.

And it wasn't just metal. Something was wrong with it. It was deeply unnatural. Evil, even. Podkin watched as the odd snowflake hit its surface and vanished with a sudden hiss.

'What ... what *is* that?' he whispered to Paz. Whispering, not because he was afraid of waking the Gorm, but because he didn't want to draw the attention of that thing. Some part of him wondered why he was stupid enough to think a lump of iron was alive, but every instinct told him that it was.

'It's like that thing we saw at Redwater.' Paz's voice was small and scared. 'But much bigger. And more powerful, I think. See what it's doing to those rabbits.'

Podkin tore his eyes away from the metal and looked beyond it. There, arms chained out to each side, were two rabbits. They had been left,

exposed to the iron, staring at it for Goddess knows how long.

Podkin could see the effect it was having on them. Rusty clouds of blood were starting to cover the whites of their eyes. They were motionless, like statues; they looked unable to speak or think. Unable to do anything but stare at the pillar of metal.

'They're turning into *them*,' Podkin whispered. 'Into the Gorm.'

'This must be what happens – how rabbits turn into the Gorm,' said Mish. The thought made everyone tremble with horror.

'I can feel its power,' Crom agreed. 'I can feel it pulling at me, even though I can't see it. We should move on.'

The rabbits started to back away from the thing, even as it tried to draw them closer. It was a magnet, of a sort. A polluting, poisonous magnet that seemed to take over your mind. It made Podkin feel almost sorry for the Gorm, if that was possible. Once upon a time, they must have been normal rabbits, just like him. Was that the thing they dug up in their warren? The thing that changed them? He supposed it could have happened to any rabbit. Maybe even Munbury itself, if it had been built near a seam of that warped metal.

As they stepped away from it, Podkin was sure he saw it shudder – a ripple in the solid iron, and something vaguely eye-like blinking out at him. He felt Starclaw grow suddenly heavier – hotter in his hand. As if the blade were angry again.

But, in the next instant, both blade and pillar were still lifeless metal again. Had he imagined the whole thing? *Concentrate*, he told himself. *Get your head together, Podkin. You're in the middle of a Gorm camp, two whiskers away from being skinned alive, for Goddess's sake!*

'Come on! We have to hurry!' Paz hissed. Podkin pulled himself back to the present. They were far enough from the iron that its power was weaker. Holding each others' paws in a line, the rabbits broke free completely and rushed over to the prisoners' enclosure.

As they neared it, the thought of seeing his mother again made Podkin step faster and faster, until he was running across the trampled snow, dagger held out before him.

He reached the pen and chopped straight through the fence. There were the prisoners, bundled together in a huge mass of bodies, trying to keep out the cold.

'Mother! Mother!' Podkin cried and now the sight of them up close caused Podkin to gasp in horror.

These were starved rabbits – sorry things, more dead than alive. Their fur was patchy and dull; skin hung from their bones, and their eyes were blank orbs in deep shadowy sockets. Even though their pen was broken and they were free to escape, they barely moved. Their heads followed the little form of Podkin as they blinked stupidly at him.

'Mother!' he called again. 'It's Podkin! Has anyone seen my mother? Lady Enna from Munbury? Or Olwyn?'

There were dull groans from the huddle, which didn't even sound like words. And then Paz was with him, both of them calling out for their mother together.

Finally, just when Podkin was beginning to think it had all been for nothing, there was a muttering from the centre of the huddle. The bodies began to rise, to move aside, and two rabbits came staggering out towards them. Podkin felt Paz grasp his arm and squeeze it, and they both held their breath as the weakened rabbits came closer. They were dressed in rags and blankets. Slowly, the moonlight lit their haggard faces, and Podkin could see brown fur: filthy, matted and patchy, but the same colour as his mother's and aunt's at least. Could it really be?

'Mother!' Paz shouted – the first to completely recognise them. 'Mother!'

A spark of light and recognition appeared in the empty eyes of the starved rabbits, and Podkin saw his mother and his aunt come back to themselves like frozen flowers thawing in the sunlight.

'Children? Is it you?' The voice was cracked and broken, but it was definitely his mother's. Podkin didn't remember running to her, but in the next instant he was wrapped in the fiercest, tightest hug he had ever known, with Paz and his aunt all crushed together as well. He could feel hot tears running out of his eyes, and he heard a wailing and sobbing that was part joy, part sorrow and seemed to come from everywhere at once.

It was wonderful.

Which made it all the more terrible when it was shattered by the sharp cawing of a Gorm crow.

Podkin's eyes snapped upwards, searching the black sky for the bird. But Mish and Mash were quicker. There was a flurry of *zips* as their slingshot and blowpipe fired in quick succession, and then three or four feathered shapes crashed out of the sky, smacking into the snowy ground with meaty thumps.

Crom had his spear and shield ready. 'We have to go. *Now.*' Wherever there were birds, the Gorm weren't far away. And any second now their sleeping comrades inside the camp might also wake up. If they didn't move quickly they would find themselves surrounded.

But it was too late.

Behind them, beside that awful pillar, the two chained creatures, half-Gorm, half-rabbit, started moaning. A low, tortured sound, as if something was causing them great and terrible pain. Podkin could feel the thing thrumming and throbbing, growing frantic with rage and excitement.

It was almost as though it were calling out to someone or something, Podkin thought, gritting his teeth so hard he thought they would crack. *But what?*

He had a sick certainty that he knew, but he didn't want to believe it was possible. Instead, he pulled at his mother's arm, hoping to get her away from this terrible place before they were parted again.

And that was when the camp gates burst open.

With a crash and a flurry of snow, a pack of riders stormed through the gateway, the pounding of their iron-clad beasts making the ground shake. They thundered *through* the campfire, sending a tsunami of orange sparks skittering across the snow; they galloped past the jagged metal pillar, which cried out in horrible glee, and finally they skidded to a halt in a wash of steam and melted snow, with a screeching of metal against metal that made all the other rabbits clutch their ears.

'You.' A voice came out of the clouds, cold and flat and metallic. The voice of something that would eat you alive, just because you were in its way.

Podkin knew that voice. He could never forget it. It was the one he heard every night in his nightmares, the voice from the last night he saw his father alive.

He peered out from the huddle of cold furry bodies, looking up to see a huge Gorm rabbit, the lopsided metal horns of his armour twisted up above his head like an evil iron version of Hern himself.

It was Scramashank.

*

'You. Boy.' The voice spoke again, and somehow, even though every scrap of flesh in his little body told him not to, Podkin found himself stepping forward, out in front of Scramashank, with Starclaw held before him in his shaking hands. The dagger was buzzing gently, reminding him of its power, although even that didn't make him feel any braver.

'You must be the runt we have been looking for. The runaway kitten from Munbury. Fancy that – searching up and down the whole of Enderby, and here you are, walking right into our camp with the *real* magic dagger in your hands. Is it a gift for me, bratling? A thank-you present for killing your stupid father?' Scramashank sounded as though he was smiling behind the iron faceplate of his helm. The kind of smile that used all of your teeth and made your eyes look as though they were about to pop out of your head.

'Leave him be.' Crom's voice came from behind him and, without looking back, Podkin knew the blind rabbit was moving into a fighting stance, ready to give his life. 'Pick a fight with *me*, if you've got the whiskers.'

Scramashank turned his head slightly, and in that instant Podkin knew he would kill Crom without so much as a blink.

'Stay back, Crom!' Podkin moved a step closer to the Gorm riders. 'That's an order! Stay back!'

Despite being bigger, older and scarier than the little rabbit, Crom found himself obeying. He was a soldier after all, down to the bone, and Podkin was a chieftain by right. He stepped back, leaving Podkin standing on his own - a tiny scrap of a rabbit clutching a dagger that was too big for him.

Podkin heard sounds of protest from Paz, his mother and his aunt, but he ignored them. Out of the corner of his eye, he saw the little shapes of Mish and

Mash running away from the Gorm, out of the camp. He couldn't really blame them.

'Yes, I have the dagger!' He wanted his voice to sound strong and unafraid. Like his father's when he had faced Scramashank. Instead it came out weak and shaky, but still he carried on. 'This is it. This is Starclaw. What do you want with it?'

'To destroy it, of course. To destroy all of the Twelve Gifts, like I did the sacred helmet of Sandywell.' Scramashank made a crushing motion with his fist, and behind him the iron pillar groaned in hunger.

'But why?' said Podkin. 'I don't understand. Why would you want to destroy something so special? What good will it do you?'

Scramashank snorted and made a motion towards his sword hilt, as if he were going to kill Podkin there and then. But in the end he couldn't resist the chance to boast. After all, he did have a captive audience.

'The Balance,' he said. 'Have you heard of it? The balance between our master and nature. Neither can become too powerful. But if the Twelve Gifts are destroyed, then there will be no Balance. No more tribes, no more petty feasts and pointless festivals. There will be only the Gorm.'

It began to make sense to Podkin. The Gorm were like a disease, like a virus. They wanted to spread themselves across all the Five Realms until there was nothing else left. He felt anger like a fire burning in his little belly. Before he knew it, he couldn't stop himself.

'But that's just wrong,' he said. 'What about the Goddess? What about all the other gods and goddesses and spirits and everything else? Who says that being Gorm is the right way? Why should you get to take us all over, just because you've got that stupid iron armour? It's just ... it's just ... not *fair*!'

Scramashank sat atop his mount and stared down at Podkin for a heartbeat, then two. The little rabbit thought, for one hopeful instant, that his words might have pierced through the iron armour controlling whoever was inside. Could the chieftain, or the rabbit he was before, still be alive in there somewhere? Could he be listening, fighting against the poison in his mind and trying to return?

But when Scramashank spoke again, his voice was as cold and heartless as before.

'You rabbits don't understand the glory and strength of the Gorm. How could you? I used to be a pathetic timid failure of a chieftain, always doubting myself, always scared of making the wrong decision. Walking around with that oversized copper pot on my head like a fool.

'Now I have no doubts. No weaknesses. No fear. All I have is power and purpose. You puny things of flesh and fur don't understand. This entire world belongs to Gormalech. He was cheated of it, but he will have it back. It will be washed clean for him in a tide of blood and iron, along with all your tribes, gods and goddesses.'

As though in response to his words, the metal pillar howled. Podkin clearly saw spikes and jagged hooks pushing up from beneath its surface. The Gorm around him writhed on their saddles, some of them cackling and whooping with joy. These things could never be reasoned with. They were pure evil, lost to all sense and blind to everything that was good in the world.

That was when Podkin snapped. Never mind that he wasn't even half the Gorm Lord's size. Never mind that his magic weapon was totally useless against him. He pulled himself up as tall as he could and shouted at the top of his voice.

'Fight me then, *Smell-a-skank*, and you'll see just what real rabbits are made of! Or run me down with your stupid iron monster! I don't care. I am Podkin, son of Lopkin, chieftain of Munbury warren, and you are nothing but a fat, stinking coward!'

With the fiercest roar he could manage, he launched himself at Scramashank's mount and began whacking his dagger against its head-armour, just below the thing's left eye.

Clang! Clang! Clang! Scramashank stared down at him, bemused. 'Your knife doesn't cut through iron, idiot,' he said. 'You won't be able to kill my beast like that.'

Podkin ignored him and kept on striking. 'I'm not trying to kill it . . .' *clang!* 'I'm just . . .' *clang!* 'showing . . .' *clang!* 'my friend where to throw . . .' *clang!* 'his spear!'

There was a whistling sound, followed by a wet

squidgy *thunk*. One second the beast was glaring down at the frenzied Podkin below, the next there was a two-metre-long ash spear jutting out of its eye socket. With a strangled yelp, it collapsed to the floor, sending Scramashank toppling into the snow.

There was a cheer from Podkin's family and the prisoners behind them, which was quickly cut off by the other Gorm raising their own spears. That and the horrible sight of Scramashank rising slowly, unstoppably to his feet again.

His red eyes flashing, the Gorm Lord came striding around the body of his dead mount. In his hands was his huge broadsword, and he looked more terrifying and murderous than any rabbit ever has, before or since.

Oh whiskers, Podkin thought. *What shall I do now?* In his imagination, Scramashank should have been trapped underneath the iron beast, and then they could somehow all have run away. He'd never thought he'd actually have to *fight* the monster.

Remember. A voice rang in his head. It sounded a lot like his father – that gentle, lecturing voice he used to use when he was trying to tell Podkin how to be a good chieftain. *Remember what Crom taught you. You can't cut his armour, but you can block a little. And you're much smaller and faster. Now, quick! Duck, roll and jump!*

Podkin didn't need to be told twice. With a yelp, he dived right between the legs of Scramashank and rolled out the other side, ducking low as the Gorm Lord swung his sword round behind.

Armour clanked, and Scramashank spun to face Podkin. Pod flipped backwards, out of reach, and the sword thudded into the ground.

'You can't jump around forever, rat-maggot.' Scramashank sounded almost amused, sure of his eventual victory. 'Soon you will get tired, and then I will peel you like a parsnip.'

'Not yet, you won't!' Podkin dashed left and right. He hopped and sidestepped and feinted, all the while keeping just out of reach of the deadly sword blade. From the corner of his eye, he could see Crom and Paz hefting their weapons, ready to jump in and come to his aid.

Boots! That voice again, only this time more urgent. He rolled under a particularly low sword-swipe, wondering what his mind was telling him.

Boots? What about them? And then it came to him.

Scramashank's boots weren't iron. They were leather. Big black leather boots. That meant Starclaw could . . .

He just happened to be standing between the Gorm Lord's legs. Without a second thought, he swung the dagger sideways, aiming for the spot above Scramashank's ankle. It *swished* through, as if it were nothing more than a blade of grass.

There was a roar of agony somewhere above his head, and something splattered all over the snow: crimson on white. Podkin smelt a hot iron stink and heard the hiss of rapidly melting ice. *Blood*, he thought, and then Scramashank collapsed in a heap, clutching his leg and screaming so loud it hurt Podkin's ears. For the first time, he sounded like a real animal.

The little rabbit looked up to see the rest of the Gorm riders turning towards him, spears raised. *This is it*, he thought. *I'm going to be skewered like a hedgehog.*

But instead there was an explosion from the direction of the iron pillar. A flower of orange light and a roar that drowned out Scramashank's howls. It was followed by another, and another.

The glare made Podkin's eyes water, and the noise rang in his ears. For a moment he thought the world itself was ending, and then he saw Mish and Mash running amongst the Gorm, waving lit torches and shouting. *Of course*, Podkin realised. *'Bang dust.' Their plan was to blow up the Gorm camp. His friends weren't fleeing – they were setting up bombs!*

The effect on the Gorm mounts was dramatic. With their riders clinging on for dear life, they turned and stampeded across the camp, crashing into each other with great clangs of iron.

'Well done, little one.' Crom was beside him, one big paw on his shoulder, and his sword drawn. 'But we are not safe yet.'

'Wait!' Mish was pointing out of the camp, in the direction of the hill where they had left Brigid and Pook. 'What's that?'

All eyes turned up to the hillside, where the silhouette of a tall robed rabbit could be seen, her arms raised high. Brigid! As they watched, a bank of rolling mist swept up behind her like a cresting wave, and then crashed on to the hillside, flowing up and over the camp walls and covering everything within.

Podkin and the others stood, transfixed, as the fog washed over them. It was cool and sweet, and Pod could smell fresh pine sap, spring leaves and summer dew, all mixed into one.

But the Gorm weren't so keen. As soon as the mist touched them, they fell to the ground, choking, gasping and clutching at their throats. Their already terrified beasts toppled over, trampling and crushing them into the snow.

Podkin looked across to where the iron pillar stood, now lopsided after Mish and Mash's blast of bang dust. He thought he saw it writhing and twisting. As the fog continued to wash over them, he *might* have seen the soil around the pillar burst open with bright green roots and brambles that reached up their thick hungry tendrils to wrap it and drag it down under the wet dark earth.

Whatever actually happened, when the mist

cleared a little, the horrid thing had gone, leaving nothing but a scar on the ground.

And then Paz was shaking him, shouting in his face. 'Podkin, you were amazing! Just like a real chieftain!' She grabbed him in a quick, fierce hug, and then there was a blur of everything happening at once.

The prisoners were properly awake now, all running for the camp gates with Mish and Mash trying to herd them in the right direction. Crom had Podkin's mother under one arm, his aunt under the other. At some point, Brigid and Pook had come down from the hill; there they were, holding hands with Mish and running along with everyone else.

Someone had brought over the wagon tethered to the mangy rat, and they were loading it with prisoners too sick to walk, and then they were all running and stumbling out of the camp and back in the direction of the forest.

Podkin looked back, still not sure whether he was dreaming. Scramashank had stopped moving, passed out cold. The body of his iron beast was nearby and, on the ground in front of Pod, his boot, complete with foot inside.

I should probably take that with me, Podkin thought, half in a daze. *Might be lucky.*

'Did I really do that?' he managed to say.

'You did, little brother.' Podkin looked up to see Paz gazing back at him proudly. It was the first time he could remember her looking at him like that. 'Don't let it go to your head, though,' she added. 'You're still an annoying little weasel-brain.'

His mother safe. His father avenged. A new home waiting for them all in the forest ... Podkin's feet were as light as moonbeams and his grin as bright as starlight as he sheathed his magic dagger and ran south with his sister beside him, both of them faster than the wind.

CHAPTER SIXTEEN

The End of the Beginning

The bard finishes speaking, and then places his hands together and bows – the sign that the story is done.

At first the little rabbits cheer, happy that Podkin has triumphed, and the adults around the room clap; but then the questions begin, tumbling out one over another as the rabbits rush to speak.

'What happened next?'

'Was Scramashank dead?'

'Was Podkin's mother all right?'

'Was that the end of the Gorm?'

'Did they all go back to Darkhollow?'

The bard lets the questions wash over him, before raising his hands. Gradually, the little rabbits stop chirping and sit in silence again.

'Those are all good questions,' he says. 'But the stories that answer them are for another night. I believe it's time for little ones to be abed, or the Midwinter Rabbit won't be visiting this warren.'

'Will you be here tomorrow night?' one tired rabbit asks. The bard looks over at Chief Hubert, who claps his hands and nods his head, smiling broadly.

'It appears I will,' says the bard. 'And perhaps a few nights longer. At least until the winter solstice is done.'

The little rabbits cheer, and one by one get up from the hearth and go to find their parents. In the end, just two are left: the inquisitive rabbit and the sensible one.

'I still don't get it,' says the inquisitive rabbit. 'All the stories about Podkin are about how brave and strong and powerful he was. In your one he was just a scared little rabbit. Just like one of us.'

'That,' says the bard, 'is exactly what he was. Just

like one of you. You don't have to be brave or strong or powerful to do incredible things.'

'And what's the point,' the little rabbit continues, 'of just telling that bit of the story? I want to hear about Podkin's ragtag army, and how he beats the Gorm for good, forever, and everything else.'

'Stories have beginnings, they have middles and they have endings,' says the bard. 'That was just the end of the beginning.'

'Well, I think it was a good story,' says the sensible rabbit. The bard smiles his thanks. 'A *very* good story.'

'Kind of you to say so.'

'It was realistic.'

'I like to think so.'

'It was *very* realistic. Almost too realistic ...'

'Are you getting to a point?' the bard asks. 'Only, I'd like a flagon or two of mead now, and perhaps some more soup.'

'My point,' says the sensible rabbit, 'is that you know an awful lot of details about Podkin. More than anybody should know unless they were *actually there.*'

'What are you saying?' says the bard, a mischievous smile playing on his face.

The inquisitive rabbit's eyes turn as wide as soup bowls. 'What? Really? Do you think the bard is Podkin? Do you think Podkin's become a wandering storyteller?'

The bard doesn't say a word.

'Well,' says the sensible rabbit. 'He hasn't taken his hood off since he got here. Why else would he keep it on, unless he was hiding his missing ear?'

The bard gives a chuckle and reaches up for his hood. The two rabbits hold their breath as he pulls it back to reveal . . . two normal ears, tattooed in blue swirls like the rest of his dyed fur.

'I'm flattered you think I could be Podkin,' says the bard. 'But I'm afraid I'm not he. The story was told to me, and my bard's memory filled it with little things that made it real. Everyday details. Feelings and sensations. Nothing but a piece of storytelling magic.'

The sensible rabbit's face falls and his friend punches him lightly on the arm for being so stupid. Despite their blushes, the two disappointed rabbits remember to say their goodnights and shuffle off to sleep in their burrows. The bard receives a hearty slap on the back from Hubert and a fresh flagon of mead, and then makes his way to the edge of the longburrow. The musicians have the fireside now, and it is time for the parents to dance the Bramble Reel and sing the old songs. No place for an aging storyteller.

He picks his way through the shadows until he finds a bench tucked away in an alcove. There is already another rabbit there. An old one: sitting, whittling a piece of wood by the light of a candle. The bard takes a seat next to him and raises his flagon in a toast.

'Midwinter blessings.'

'And to you,' says the old rabbit. 'Nice story.'

'Thank you,' says the bard.

'You didn't have to make me sound like such a brat, though.'

The bard looks at the aged, wrinkled rabbit with his greying fur and wispy beard. He takes in his watery eyes, trembling hands and the faint marks of old scars here and there. He looks like any ancient old warrior that could be found in the corner of any warren throughout the whole Five Realms.

Except he isn't.

The bard laughs and pulls his older brother to him in a fierce hug, careful not to dislodge the false ear tied to the side of his head. 'Your memory is fading, Pod. You were the biggest brat of all.'

'I suppose I was. I'm glad to see you, Pook.'

'I'm glad to see you too. It's been too many Midwinters.'

'That it has.'

The two brothers sit together then, listening in silence as the music fills the longburrow and the singing and dancing run on into the night. They sit and hold hands and think about Midwinters past, the stories in between and how, on a night like this – once upon a time – everything changed forever.